HOT
IN
DECEMBER

JOE R. LANSDALE

DRP

Dark Regions Press
2013

LIMITLESS TRADE PAPERBACK EDITION

Cover design © 2013 by Keri Knutson

Editor & Publisher, Chris Morey
Line editor, Emma Audsley

Interior design by F.J. Bergmann
fibitz.com
ISBN: 978-1-62641-014-5

Dark Regions Press LLC
6635 N. Baltimore Ave.
Portland, OR 97203
United States of America

darkregions.com

For Karen and Keith

"I reckon a body that ups and tells the truth when he is in a tight place is taking considerable many risks ..."

—*Huckleberry Finn*, Mark Twain

One

Life-and-death issues sometimes start as simple things.

We were out in the backyard, me and my wife, and I was standing at the barbecue grill with a spatula in my hand, wearing a faded apron with *KISS THE COOK* written across it. I had managed to get a few burger patties off the grill, catching only one of them on fire and turning it black as a lump of coal. I like to grill now and again, but I'm no good at it, and I was thinking about that when I heard a car squeal around the corner.

Leaning around the edge of the house, I looked over the fence and out at the street just in time to see the car make the corner with a scream of tires and a grind of gears, and that's when I saw the car hit the woman crossing the street with her dog. Hit her with a sound that made me sick to my stomach.

From where I was standing I had a good look at the car and the driver, and I saw the woman try to jump back, jerking the dog on the leash as she did, but it was too late. The car hit her and knocked her flying out of my sight.

I threw down the spatula, pushed my wife Kelly aside, jumped over a Big Wheel, charged through the back door and through the house and out the front. The car was gone, but the woman was knocked up in our yard and her arm was twisted in a funny way behind her head and one leg was thrown up high and over her shoulder. Her jeans were halfway torn off and she had lost a shoe. I hadn't realized it when I saw the accident, my eyes being locked

1

on the driver for some reason, but I knew her. We all knew each other on that block. It was Madeline Roan; Maddy, we all called her, a vivacious redhead, what in the old days they used to call a looker, and about as nice a person as you could want to meet.

It didn't take a doctor to know at first sight that she was dead. Thirty-five years old and crossing the little street that parted our subdivision, and she was dead as a brick.

I saw the dog had been missed and was cowering across the way, lying down with its belly against the grass in the yard that belonged to the Roans. The dog was a white miniature poodle named Yip, and I have no idea how it avoided being run over and killed as well.

It was December, but in East Texas the weather was hot as fresh-poured asphalt. In contrast, the streets and yards and houses were decorated with Christmas lights, snowmen, Santas in sleighs, the usual holiday riggings. People were coming out of their air-conditioned houses to see what had happened. I had moved over close to Maddy, hoping to be wrong, that she would just have a broken arm and leg.

I wasn't wrong. Her eyes were already going glassy. Her mouth was open slightly and there was blood in one corner and saliva in the other. There were grass stains along the side of one cheek. There wasn't a wound that I could see, but my guess was the inside of her body was in the condition of a glass shop after a tornado had blown through it. In her left hand was a plastic bag. It took me a moment to put that together, but then I realized she had it there so she could pick up her dog's poop with it, turn it outside in and have it ready for the trash.

Her husband, Ross, came out of their house then, came running across the street, screaming so high-pitched it was as if he were a panther. By that time Kelly had come out of our home, seen what had happened and gone back inside to dial 911. I was glad our little daughter, Sue, was away visiting her grandmother. It was traumatic enough for a grown person, but a child …

The car that had killed Maddy wasn't present. It was long gone.

It seemed like forever and a day before the ambulance got there and the cops came moseying up to our yard. There were several of them, and they went this way and that, looking for her shoe, photographing the street to see if there were tire marks, I suppose. There weren't any. The driver hadn't made any kind of attempt to slow down. He had been gearing up as he made the corner, not gearing down.

They loaded poor Maddy in an ambulance, though the emergency was long past, and then two of the cops in plain clothes came over to see me. Behind them, across the way, I could see Ross near-collapsed on the curb in front of his house, crying savagely. The poor guy sounded like a torture victim, and I guess in a way, he was. Yip was in his lap, shaking like he had some kind of vibrator up his ass. There were two cops with Ross. One standing, one sitting by his side on the curb, about halfway holding him up.

I invited the cops in the house and without really thinking about it offered them coffee. Kelly offered them something else, juice, water. We didn't seem to know how to talk to them about seeing our neighbor killed, didn't know how to act. Death I had seen, but this kind of thing, a neighbor and her dog crossing the street, getting hit by a car for no good reason other than whoever was in the car was driving too fast, that was different.

I wondered if the cops were used to that kind of thing, stunned people. Maybe they were just as shocked as we were. Laborde was a good-sized town, a small city, so it's possible they had seen a lot more than I thought.

Kelly offered them a spot on the couch, and when we were all sitting, one of the cops, who was wearing a dark, loose shirt with a square-cut bottom, leaned forward with his elbows on his knees, said his name was Lt. Ernest and asked us our names and asked if we saw what happened.

Kelly said she hadn't, but I had, and I told them what I saw.

"Do you know what she was doing?" Ernest asked.

"Walking her dog," I said. "Far as I could tell."

They nodded.

"Can you identify the car, Mr. Chan?"

3

"I can," I said. "It was a blue Cadillac. I don't know what year. I don't know cars that well."

The other man, who was fat and wearing a Hawaiian shirt and looked like his feet hurt and so did his job, said, "What about the driver, you get a look at him?"

"I did," I said. "I saw him really well. It seemed like his face was close to me. It wasn't, but it seemed that way. Adrenaline, I guess. But I got a look. A man, in his twenties, kind of dark-looking."

"Hispanic?"

"I don't think so," I said. "Maybe, but I don't think so."

"So you can identify him if you saw him again?" the dark shirt cop said.

"I can … I didn't catch your name."

"Sorry," he said. "I didn't give it. Sergeant Allen. You knew the victim?"

"Sure," I said.

"She was our next door neighbor," Kelly said. "Jesus, no one's supposed to drive like that, that fast. Not here in the subdivision, there are signs everywhere."

I looked down. My hands were trembling.

"She has a daughter, our daughter's age," Kelly said. "It's not fair."

"No," said Allen, "it isn't."

Two

They asked us to come downtown, give an official on-record statement, and we did. I drove, but I don't recall the drive. I faintly remember the Christmas banners and lights that hung over the streets in preparation for the holidays, but considering what had just happened, they seemed surreal, out of place, like some kind of cruel cosmic joke. Next thing I remember we were walking past the dispatcher, a little man with a bald head. He looked up at us, and then Lieutenant Ernest was there, beckoning to us, and a moment later we were in a small room that was a little too warm. There was a large window that looked out at the hall in the police station, and there was a table and some folding chairs. There was a little counter and some cabinets above it. There was a pot of coffee on the counter, and I could smell how stale the coffee was from across the room. The odor made my stomach feel sick. I looked down at the table. Some wiseass, probably being interrogated, had carved his name in the table with something sharp. It read *Leonard*.

Sergeant Allen brought in some thick books, said, "He may not be in here. Good chance our guy is just some idiot who chose to drive too fast for whatever reason and fate caught up with him today, not to mention your poor neighbor. But it might be someone that's been in trouble. Seems someone starts out in trouble, they tend to stay in trouble. We could set you in front of the computer, let you scan that, but I still think the books are best."

He put the books down in front of me. Kelly, who was sitting

5

by me, reached out and took hold of my arm. I patted it. The books were stacked on top of each other. I pushed them aside and took one off the top and started looking.

There were some scary-looking people in there. Kind that look like they did just what you think they did. There were others who looked like their high-school yearbook pictures had been put in there by mistake. But mostly they all looked startled, like they had been caught with their hands in their pants.

Lieutenant Ernest came in and sat down at the table, then got up and got some coffee and sat back down. He suddenly seemed to remember his manners, asked if we wanted coffee. We didn't. I kept looking through the books, but didn't recognize anybody.

Then, I swear, on the last page of the last book, there he was. He looked a little younger, but it was him. The dark-skinned guy, Italian-looking, or maybe just richly tanned. Dark hair, dark eyes. I said, "This one."

I turned the book around and the two cops looked at it.

"Well," said Ernest. "Well, well."

"You know him?" I said.

"Oh yeah. He's part of what you might call a crime family. We're not talking mafia, well, maybe Dixie Mafia, the redneck equivalent, but they're bad enough. What's left of them around here. They used to have a slick boy named Cox ran it all, but his son got him in some shit over a girl, and so on. Couple of tough boys from here, private investigators of a sort, caught up with him. They helped put him away and they aren't even cops."

"They're meddlers," said Allen.

"Yeah, but that's neither here nor there," Ernest said. "Thing is, the organization got taken over by a fellow named Pye Anthony."

"They don't need to know all that," Allen said.

"Yeah," Ernest said. "They do. Here's the thing, you identify this fellow, then you got to do it in court."

"Okay," I said.

"Just listen," Ernest said. "So, you do that. Eyewitness identifications aren't taken as seriously as they once were. All those doubts about how people say they saw someone for sure, and then DNA proves it wasn't them."

"It was him," I said.

"I believe you," Ernest said. "I believe he ran over that woman because he was out joyriding where he shouldn't have been, drunk would be my guess, or just didn't give a damn, or a combination of both. He ran over her and kept right on going. You identify him, we might be able then to connect the car. We see if it's got a dent or two, maybe some DNA from the dead lady in the grillwork, caught up the tires. Maybe with that we can make a case. I think we can. It's not like he's going to look good on the stand, all the things he's been into. He's already got a past, some of it dealing with cars, stolen ones, ones he wrecked drunk driving. So he's got a history, a dark one. That works in our favor."

"You're talking a lot," Allen said.

"I'm talking more than I normally should," Ernest said, "but I want Mr. and Mrs. Chan to know where I'm coming from, why I'm telling them this. You see, these people are bad people. I mean really bad people. I don't mean they talk bad language or spit on the sidewalk or pee in someone's soup when they aren't looking. You testify against them, they're not going to like it. Pye Anthony isn't going to like it especially, because the man you identified is Will Anthony, and he's Pye's son."

"Are you saying we're in danger?" Kelly asked.

"Pye is not a nice man, but I'm thinking we can put some police on your house, some protection. You won't need it until we arrest him, maybe not even then, but when it's clear who's going to come forward and point a finger at him, well, maybe then. You see what I'm talking about?"

"Yeah," I said. "I see."

"You'll still testify?"

"Yes," I said.

"All right," Ernest said, nodding like he was trying to shake his head off his neck. "We'll see if we can set up a line-up, and you come in and see if you can still identify him. I just want you to know what

7

you're doing."

"Christmas holidays are coming up," Allen said. "Your little girl, you could put her somewhere safe, maybe keep her with the grandmother, and we could put some guards on the house, that kind of thing, and once we got him nailed, we'll push for a speedy trial, telling the judge the situation, and we can maybe get the guy nailed quick."

"Does it ever work like that?" Kelly said. "Swift justice?"

"Now and again," Ernest said. "I'll ask you again. You still want to testify?"

I thought about Maddy, the way she had been knocked through the air, the wreck of her body. The face of that driver, not so much concerned or frightened, but more like some kid with a video game, knocking down the last warrior, heading for home.

"Sure," I said. "I'll identify him. I'll testify."

Three

We went past the bald dispatcher again, out to our car, and then home, and by the next day they had hauled Will Anthony in for a lineup. It was all just a formality, really. I had already identified him on the page, but they wanted to see if I was sure, so they'd have all their ducks in a row. I was asked to drive over, and then I went in and sat in darkness, looked through a one-way glass and it was easy. The others were kind of the same build and look, but it was him, Will Anthony, the guy in the photo.

Later, back in the coffee room, with just me and Lieutenant Ernest and a cup of bad coffee apiece, he said, "They don't know who you are, but you ought to watch yourself, and if it gets down to it, you can change your mind and back out, you feel you should."

"I'm fine," I said. "You work for the law or not?"

"I do," he said. "But I'm a father first."

"Wouldn't Pye be after you too? You're one helping send Will to jail. I mean, more you than me, actually."

"They know we're their adversaries. Kill me, another cop steps up and takes my place. They get rid of you, well, no testifying, no saying in court 'that's the man,' and if we don't have that, we have a car he repaired, a bad rap sheet and no eyewitness. So you could be putting your nuts in the blender. See what I'm saying."

"But you are offering me protection?"

"I am, but we're cops, and there's a limit to what we can do and how long we can do it. We're not the National Guard."

Something in that made me more than a little concerned, but I said, "I'll still testify."

"Then it's done," Ernest said.

Four

Kelly and I were at the sink. I was rinsing the dinner dishes and she was putting them in the dishwasher.

"You sure you want to do this?" Kelly said. She was talking to me like I was one of her kindergarten students. "Lieutenant Ernest sounded less than certain about protecting us."

"What about Maddy? What about her child?"

"What about us?" Kelly said, pausing with a dish in her hand. "What about our child?"

My stomach boiled a little.

"We'll be all right," I said.

"Would you bet your life on that?" Kelly said.

"Mine, not yours or Sue's."

"Betting yours means you're betting ours," she said, put the dish in the washer, closed it up, and went upstairs. I stood there with dishes still in the sink. I rinsed them and opened up the washer, put them in, poured myself a cup of coffee, sat at the table and thought about things. The coffee went cold in the cup.

Will Anthony did it. Ran over Maddy like she was a chicken crossing the road. Accident, on purpose, whatever, he did it and didn't care, didn't stop. I didn't testify, he'd get away. I had protection promised, but what was their protection worth? One man in a car sleeping out front? Maybe sleeping on the couch. Another cop in the backyard, if the budget allowed?

And what would happen after Will was convicted? What if

he wasn't convicted? The old man, would he hold a grudge either way? Some people lived by the feud. I had known a guy in the war, over in Afghanistan, and this Afghan kid had made some kind of gesture or face at him. I don't know. I didn't see it happen. He told me about it, and he was burnt up by it. Stuff like how we were there for them, and it wasn't appreciated.

I was there because I was in the army to get the opportunity to get an education as a helicopter pilot. I got it, never used it, bought out a guy's frame shop in downtown Laborde instead. But this guy, I think he went back and killed that kid. I don't know for sure he did, but I know they found a kid dead, and his tongue had been cut out. I got to thinking maybe the kid stuck out his tongue at him and the guy just couldn't let it pass. I don't know. I told my CO about it, but there wasn't a thing could be proved, just speculation.

There was this other guy in our unit at the time, Cason Statler, and it was on my mind, so I told him and a buddy of his, guy they called Booger, what my suspicions were. Booger was what you might call a sociopath, or in East Texas terms, a bad son of a bitch. I shouldn't have said a thing in front of him. He didn't care for anyone. Except Cason. Not sure why, but he loved the guy like a brother. Next day they found the soldier I told them about dead with his tongue cut out, same as the kid. I always thought it was my loose mouth got him killed. What if that guy didn't do the murder? What if I was wrong? I think what got him done in was when I spoke to Cason, Cason said something like, "Bastard did that doesn't deserve to wear the uniform and ought to pay for what he did."

I figured Booger, hearing that, did the killing for Cason, or at least it was that way in his mind. He went out and found the soldier and killed him and cut his tongue out, pinned it to the soldier's chest with a pocket knife. No one could prove anything. I just hoped I was right about that soldier being guilty.

Thinking on that made me think about Cason. Me and him had been pretty good friends, on account of we were both from East Texas, him being from a town not far over from Laborde. After the war I didn't try to keep up with him, and he didn't try to keep up with me. Maybe there were too many old memories there, things we didn't want to dredge up, so I hadn't really wanted to see him.

Until now.

Five

I got on the internet the next day and looked to see if I could find Cason. I remembered he said he had been a journalist, so I added that into the mix. He was easy to find. He had been nominated for a Pulitzer Prize for his newspaper work in Houston, but was no longer living there. After that it was an easy jump through the internet to find out he still worked at a newspaper, but no longer in Houston. He was working at one in his home town, not that far away. Camp Rapture, an old lumber camp that had blossomed into a pretty good-sized town.

I got on the phone and called the paper, pretty sure I'd hang up when they answered, but I didn't. The receptionist asked me my business.

"I need to speak to Cason Statler."

The next moment he was on the phone.

"You remember an old desert rat?" I said.

"A bunch of them. Which one are you?"

"Tom Chan."

"Why, you old dog-dick-sucking son-of-a-bitch."

"Oh, come on, man," I said, falling right back in with our old way of joshing. "You act like that's a bad thing."

He laughed and we talked a bit, about how we had been only about twenty miles apart all this time and not knowing, and so on. I didn't mention that I had never even tried to look him up. I didn't have to. I knew he knew, and I figured he had been just the same when it came to me, but now that I had found him, it was damn near like old times, but without being shot at or worried about being blown up. We went on about this and that for a while, the war coming into it, but not too direct, and then I said, "You know, I hate to call you up like this, but I got this problem that I thought I could talk to you about. I don't know why I need to talk to you exactly, but I'm thinking I do. I'm not asking for money. I'm not asking you to do anything, other than listen. Maybe give some advice."

"You saved my bacon once, and I haven't forgotten that."

"That was me and your friend Booger," I said. "We did it together."

"Christ," Cason said. "Don't say his name. When you speak of the devil, he might appear."

"So can we talk?"

"I'm pretty flexible," he said, "being as I'm the best goddamn reporter here."

"Not bashful, are you?"

"A bashful fellow never has a chance with the ladies," he said. "And I do like the ladies."

Six

Kelly was off from school as a teacher for the Christmas holidays, but she had to go in that day to do some kind of work of her own, something to wrap up the term. Nothing official, just a day by herself in her classroom.

As she was getting ready to leave, dressed in slacks and tennis shoes, a baggy shirt and no makeup, I said, "If it's all right, I'm going to drive over to Camp Rapture and visit an old army buddy."

"An army buddy?"

"That's right."

"Male?"

"All the way."

"Why this, all of a sudden?" she asked.

"I don't know exactly," I said. "Maybe I want to ask him some advice."

"About the hit-and-run, about testifying?"

"Yeah," I said.

"Look," she eased up to me and put her hands on my shoulders. "I know I came down pretty hard last night. I mean, I'm scared. I won't kid you. But you're doing right. We'll just have to make sure the law protects us."

"Yeah," I said.

"But you still want to see your friend, you don't have to go tell him what a shitty wife I am about not supporting you, and all that."

"That's not it. Hell, you have legitimate concerns. I don't know,

17

maybe it's because me and him haven't talked in a while. Maybe it's because we shared a few things in the service. I don't know exactly why I need to see him."

She cocked her head, making her dark hair dangle to one side like a curtain. She studied my face for a moment, gradually smiled the smile I like so much. "Sure. I'll see you later. Have fun."

Kelly went on to school. I called into the frame shop, telling my assistant, Dean, I'd be out for the day, and then I drove over to Camp Rapture, listening to music all the way. I used the GPS, so the newspaper was easy to find. When I went inside, I saw Cason get up from his desk at the back, smile and start walking toward me. He looked exactly the same as I remembered, only without the uniform. A big, good-looking guy that made everyone else around him self-conscious, me included.

I stuck out my hand, but he grabbed me and hugged me.

"Good to see you," he said.

Everyone in the office looked at us. Cason said, "It's okay. Me and him have been fucking for years."

A few of the reporters laughed, a few looked offended.

He threw his arm around my shoulders and we started out. He called out as he left, "We're going to a motel for a while, right after we stop at Walmart and buy a big jar of Vaseline. We like to keep it simple, don't we, honey?"

"I suppose we do," I said.

Seven

There was a little coffee shop in the center of town, or what used to be the center back in the old days when there was a town square. It was a mixture of coffee shop and trinkets, actually, stuff from Camp Rapture's history. There were photos on the wall. An artificial Christmas tree wearing shopworn ornaments. Cason pointed at one of the photographs. It was an old black-and-white one, and from the way people were dressed, I guessed it was from the 1930s.

He tapped the glass over the photo, said, "See that woman?"

"Yeah. These days you'd call her hot."

"She's my grandmother."

"Naw," I said.

"Yep. Sunset Jones. She was a constable once. They got pictures of her all over town. She became constable because she killed the former constable, who, by the way, was her husband."

"I guess that saves on elections and divorces."

"He was a big bully. What it saved on was him raping her. He was trying when she got his gun and killed him. Did it during a tornado."

"Some gal," I said.

"She was. Here, let's get this table."

He guided me to one in the back. A waitress came over. She was about twenty-five, I guess, dark- haired and well-built. She had nice face with a very interesting, if slightly crooked nose. Cason flirted with her a little, and it didn't hurt her feelings any. He was the kind of guy that could walk into a room and girls would stick notes in his pocket with their names and numbers on it; actually, the one time we were stateside together I saw that happen when we left base to go to a bar. I didn't get any notes.

I ordered coffee. Cason ordered a breakfast. We made with some more general bullshit, and then the coffee and his late breakfast came. I showed him photographs of Kelly and Sue I had in my wallet, pulled up some on my cell phone.

"They're better than you deserve," he said, "based on looks alone."

"I know it," I said.

"Me, I got a line of girlfriends that I've left or they've left me and I got a job at a struggling newspaper, and a book I've been working on for ten years, and so far I've just about made it to page fifteen, and about two paragraphs are any good, and that's the dedication. You're doing all right, Tom."

"Thanks," I said, and we talked a little more bullshit.

While Cason ate, he looked at me over the fork that was dipping regularly into his mouth, said, "So you got something on your mind, and it isn't about your family photographs, my love life, or the niceness of the latrines we had over in Sand World."

"Oh, those were very nice," I said. "I loved peeing down a pipe."

"Well, at least they didn't make us shit down those things.... Oh, wait. They did."

We laughed. I said, "Yeah, I guess there's something else."

"Don't be shy," he said.

"All right," I said. "This is what I got."

I told him the story. When I finished, he said, "I see what you're worried about, of course. But, man, you need to do the right thing."

"I'm afraid the right thing might be the wrong thing," I said. "Right now I'm not worried. I mean, no one outside of the police know I know who was in the car. But once it gets out there, well, it could be a problem."

The waitress came back and poured us both another cup, tried to linger, but Cason didn't flirt with her this time. He wasn't rude, but she could tell he wanted her to go, so she did. I watched her go. It was a nice departure. I'm happily married, but that hasn't killed the instinct to look. That's all I do is look, all I want to do, but hell, you got to do it; it's built into the DNA.

Cason eyed me, said, "So, I haven't seen you in years.… How many?"

"I don't know, almost six years."

"Sounds about right," he said. "And you thought you'd just come to me and ask my opinion on this? Six years goes by and we don't talk, and now we're talking. Why is that, Tom?"

"I guess I just needed someone to discuss it with. Kelly, she's trying to hang tough, be with me on this, and she said she was this morning. But the other night she wasn't so sure. And frankly, I wasn't either."

"What you're saying is you don't trust the police to keep you safe."

"What I'm saying, Cason, is they talk to me like they might not be able to, like I'm taking a big chance here. It's almost like they're trying to talk me out of it."

He nodded. "First thing, let me lay this out. I know damn near all the criminals who have their nests in East Texas. I know these assholes, the father and son you're talking about, Pye and Will Anthony. I'm a reporter, remember, and believe it or not, this part of East Texas is a hotbed of drugs, prostitution and murder, and this Pye and his son are the generals. Well, a general and an over-motivated private, that being Pye's boy Will. They took over things after Cox ended up in the can. Cox thought he could hold onto it, and he would have been the better one to do it, but it didn't work out that way. He was out of sight and out of mind, and what power he had he couldn't maintain, not in jail. He didn't have access to the money there. The Anthony pair nabbed the greenbacks, and they nabbed the power. They're crafty more than smart, but when you get right down to it, it's the crafty motherfuckers you have to worry about. They don't do what's logical at any moment in time. Or if it is logical, it can go wonky out of nowhere, because they're

21

impulsive. They got a screw loose, these guys, and they got people working for them that aren't the professionals that Cox had. They know what they're doing, in the basic way. I mean they can hot-wire a car, put the right amount of talc in a batch of cocaine to soften it up and spread the dope, they can shoot straight and cut a throat as perfectly as if they laid it out with a plumb line. But they don't care who they make mad, or who they hurt, or how. They are petty. And if they are petty, think how they'll be for something this serious, the boy possibly going to prison for life, maybe even getting a needle full of poison. Manslaughter most likely. Leaving the scene of a crime, and so on. But either way, serious business. I know of one man, who crossed them in some way or another, nothing big, and they sawed off his legs with a handsaw, while he was alive. Nearly bled to death, but lived. They didn't expect him to live, but he did. He never admitted they did it, because I think he wanted to keep the rest of himself intact. Everyone in the underworld knew it, and I knew it, and the cops knew it, but the guy wouldn't say it was them. He feared they'd get to him eventually if he did. Thing was, about a year later, he was found dead in a Little League baseball field. Know what they'd done? They'd cut him up and put him in the place of home plate, just this chest and lower body. They came back on him anyway, even if he didn't talk, decided maybe they should have finished the job the first time. They found his arms in a dumpster, the hands still attached, and the hands clutching his dick, which they had superglued together. That was their way of making a joke. Not nice guys. Not nice at all."

"Damn," I said.

"Damn is right.'

"Maybe I should hire someone to protect me," I said. "Someone besides the police, someone whose job is just that, protection."

"Can you afford it?" Cason asked.

"I can."

"On a frame-shop salary?"

"It's more lucrative than you think. I also have a guy works for me, Dean, he does school photos for me. We have a number of

22

accounts, including here in Camp Rapture. People like photographs of their children, so we got that going. We also offer to frame them. It works out well. I got a bit of inherited money as well. Uncle who lived in California died, had a big batch of cash, and I ended up with part of it. Not sure how, didn't even know him that well, but that's neither here nor there. I have the money."

Cason sipped his coffee. "There's a couple of guys I wish were available, Hap Collins and Leonard Pine. I tried to get them on a simple job not long ago, for a friend, but they're out of Texas right now, doing something else. They had something to do with Cox going down, or so I hear through the grapevine. But, they're going to be gone for a while, so that won't work."

"Don't tell me about the guys I can't have," I said.

"Listen here, Tom. Here's a thought. You think it over. Like you said, you're okay right now. The beans have not been tumped over, so to speak. But you get to thinking you need help, well, there is someone."

"Oh shit," I said. "You don't mean—"

"Booger," he said. "You could get him. Pay him, he'll do the job. Have me stick with him while he does it, you'll come out without him shooting you and setting fire to your home."

"Same old Booger," I said. And I wasn't saying it with humor.

"Exactly. He's in Oklahoma. He's got a bar and a shooting range, but not in his name. He has a guy that runs it for him. He has a construction business too. He hires out now and then, and I don't mean to pour your drinks or your cement. He has other people who do that."

"I thought he'd be a felon by now," I said. "In prison."

"He would be if he'd ever been caught. So would I, frankly."

"I won't ask you about that," I said.

"And I won't talk about it. I'm only going to talk about the stuff you need to know, and here it is, same as I said before. You go home and think it over, and if you decide to testify, and I think you will, and you believe you need some security that's more than the cops, you call me. I can take off here, say I'm working on a story, throw some bullshit thing together later, and still take their breath away here at Camp Nowhere. But Booger, we got to be sure we want to bring him in. We can't just think it's a good idea, we got to know it is, because he comes loaded for bear, literally and metaphorically. Thing is, though, on something like this, should it go ugly and nasty as the devil's asshole, we want him with us. He'll dive into that hole without holding his nose if he's been paid to do it. Or he thinks I want him to. I try not to ask him to do too much, but I owe you. Come to think of it, I owe Booger too, but somehow he thinks he owes me."

"You think you owe him, and this is how you repay it?"

Cason laughed. "Don't be silly. Giving him a job like this is the kind of thing Booger calls Free Pussy."

Eight

When we got to the register to pay up, Cason took the bill and I thanked him. He flirted a little with the waitress, but she wasn't having any after the cold shoulder Cason had given her earlier. She took the money and gave him a "Thank you, sir," and we left.

Cason drove us back to the newspaper in his car, and on the way, he said, "You decide you might like some help, you call me. But if I do help you, me and Booger, you don't want that on your cell phone, pinging off towers and the like, as they can trace that, and though we can make a legitimate excuse for you calling me, why throw it in the mix? I have burners in the glove box. Call on one of those. But still, don't call from your house. Go somewhere in town if you can, use it that way. Lot of calls in town, and they don't know this number, and it's not connected to you. I use these when I'm talking to sources, sometimes people who don't want to be known. I carry a stack of the things for that reason."

I opened the glove box. There were half a dozen of the phones inside, stuffed in a plastic bag. I took one and slipped it in my pants pocket.

"Take two," Cason said. "You make a call, toss it. And if you need to make another, you got backup. You can't trace those things, you do it that way."

I took another.

"I probably won't need to call," I said. "I don't, I'll give them back."

"I hear you, but just in case. And don't worry about giving them back. Put them up somewhere, and I don't want to beat a dead horse, but if you do call, get rid of the phone. One call, you're done with it. You remember that. Get rid of it."

Well, I won't kid you, driving back to Laborde I was thinking all manner of things and none of them good. I felt a little like a citizen that had just discussed something with a foreign agent that had best been left unspoken.

Kelly was home when I got there, on the land line, talking to Sue. When I came in, she said, "Baby, want to talk to, Daddy?"

I took the phone then.

"Daddy," Sue said.

"Hey, doll. You having fun?"

"Grandma is taking me to the library."

"Checking out some books?"

"No. We're going to see a movie."

"At the library?"

After a bit of discussion, I figured out the library was showing The Little Mermaid to get kids in the door, and they were laying out books about mermaids and fairy tales and the like, hoping to get new readers. I wished them luck. Reading was one of those things everyone said they didn't have time for, but it didn't keep them from telling you the names of every trashy-ass character on reality shows.

"Okay, sweetie," I said. "You have fun. Mommy and Daddy love you."

"I love you too," she said.

When I hung up, I looked at Kelly. She was slim and beautiful and sweet-looking. Her skin was dark, a mixture of Irish, African American, and if rumor was right, Native American, Cherokee, I think. Her hair was black as midnight and so were her eyes. Sue looked like a little version of her, only plump. Looking at her, thinking of Sue, made me choke up a little.

I thought about her and Sue and the nice life we had, considered it might not be such a smart idea to testify against someone who could make that nice life uncomfortable. But I knew I was going to.

We missed Sue and talked about her for a while, as if she had moved to Mars and taken a job with the next exploration team to Jupiter. We hadn't been apart from her much, and it was hard. It didn't keep us from planning a night out, though. I figured we would be locked down for a bit after word got around I had seen Will Anthony driving the hit-and-run car and that I was going to testify against him.

Laborde isn't exactly the Mecca of great restaurants, but there's a very good Japanese place we liked. We dressed up a little fancy for a change. Kelly always looks great, and this night her jet-black hair went with the dress she wore, the classic little black dress. It was high on the leg for a kindergarten teacher, but I didn't have any complaints. I told her she looked good enough to raise the dead while I fastened the clasp of her silver necklace. I wore some dark dress pants, a light blue shirt and a dark jacket. And if I could remember what shoes I had on I'd die a happy man. Bottom line, I thought we both looked pretty snazzy.

It was about seven p.m. when we stepped outside. It was fresh dark, the street lights were on, and it was as humid as if it were mid-July. I was starting to regret the coat.

I drove us over to the restaurant. I ate sushi, and Kelly ate some kind of chicken dish with rice, and we were happy as the proverbial clams, talking about this and that on the way home, the business with poor Maddy not forgotten, but at least temporarily put on the back burner.

Upstairs we undressed, not bothering with pajamas, slowly began to touch one another, and it was a very good time. Afterward we kissed and fell asleep.

For a while there, it seemed like the perfect night.

Nine

I may have heard them, but it didn't register. I was pretty deep in sleep, and when I stirred it was to caress Kelly who was in the crook of my arm, causing it to go numb as a monk's plans for New Year's. I was gently removing it from beneath her head when the bedroom door opened and a flashlight beam hit me in the face.

I sat up quickly, but by then the beam was right on me, and then there was a blow to the side of my head that made my ears ring and knocked me back on my pillow. Then I heard Kelly scream. I tried to sit up, but I was hit again. Then Kelly made a noise that let me know she'd been hit as well.

I turned my aching head toward her. She was sitting up and the sheet had fallen away from her, revealing her nude breasts. The light jumped over her body, and the dried sweat made it gleam as if oiled. She had a hand to the side of her head. I felt something cold and metal press against my head, a voice came close to my ear, said, "You haven't done bad for yourself, have you?"

Next thing I knew we were both jerked onto the floor. Me on one side of the bed, Kelly on the other. I could tell there was more than one person in the room. I don't know if it was true instinct, or if instinct is just subtle observation you're not aware of. But I sensed more than heard movement. I was certain there was someone else when another light flashed, and I saw the light lower, like a setting moon, and realized whoever was holding it had just sat down in the chair in front of the dresser, straddling it like a horse.

29

The man in the chair said, "You and me, we could have some problems. And if I've got a problem with you, I got a problem with your wife, though I might have a bit of good feelings toward her for a little while. Maybe a long while, and then, not so much. Then I got to feel less good about her, same as you, and I know you got a daughter, too, and it could be unpleasant for her."

"What do you want?" I said. "If it's money, we haven't got much in the house. You're welcome to it."

"I have some jewelry on the dresser," Kelly said. "Take it and go."

"Frame-shop owner probably doesn't buy very expensive jewelry," the voice said. "And I don't need whatever is in your wallet. What I need is for you two to get up and get dressed, and make it snappy. We are all going for a little ride."

I was thinking don't go with them. Don't get in a car. Fight. Die here. Never go with them and never get in the car. But I couldn't do it. Not with me in the dark with my balls hanging out and them with a light in my face and holding guns, because I was pretty sure the cold metal I had felt against my head was not a curling iron. If I tried to fight, it would be a short fight, and it would be about Kelly too, and maybe something worse for her than just a bullet in the head, so I hesitated. I thought I would look for my moment. Which, of course, once you wait that long, is never going to come.

It was like when I was in the army in Afghanistan. You saw your enemy pointing a gun at you, you had to act then. You thought about it, you wouldn't be thinking long.

We got dressed in the dark. I pulled on what I had worn to dinner, minus the jacket, and Kelly pulled on the little black dress and slipped into house shoes. They made a point of shining their lights on us while we dressed, making us feel all the more vulnerable because we were nude. Then they prodded us out of there. There was a third person in the hall, and I had flashlight glimpses of faces now. One of those faces was Will Anthony, the man who had killed my next-door neighbor. My stomach seemed to sink to the floor. I knew who had us now and why.

They took us outside, right through the front door. A big car was waiting. A nice car, a big black SUV. The street lights gave it a dark green sheen. We got in the back seat, and a man who looked a lot like an older version of Will sat by Kelly; he would have been the one sitting backwards in the chair in front of the dresser. Will slid in beside me. The other man got behind the wheel. The flashlights were out by this time, and in a moment the big car was purring along. As we passed under the street lights and Christmas lights, I saw the older man put his hand on Kelly's thigh, let it rest there. My testicles seemed to shrink and the contents of my stomach turned sour.

He said, "You know who I am?"

I lied about it. "No."

"You know what, I don't believe you," he said. "But just in case you're dumber than I think. I'm Pye Anthony, and the young man with the gun in your ribs is my son, Will. He hit you in the head, I popped your sweetie here."

"Glad to meet you," I said.

Pye laughed. "No, you're not."

"You're right," I said. "I'm not."

Nothing else was said, but Pye kept running his hand along Kelly's leg. She was sitting as stiff as if she were a manikin. She turned her head slowly toward me. I can't tell you how that killed me, her looking at me, probably thinking: *Why don't you do something?* Thinking I was her big protector, and that I'd make things right, but I didn't think that was going to happen. I might die trying, but I thought that would be the best of it, a blaze of glory and a short burning fall. I had to do better than that; I had to bide my time and hope. That said, there wasn't much hope there.

The car cruised out of town to where the woods got thick, and then we took a wide road through the pines. Finally we took a broad turnoff that went through a metal framework with Anthony Construction stenciled in the metal overhang.

We were driven down the road a good piece, past a large metal building, and on out to the back of the property where we could see a bulldozer placed in the shadows.

After we parked, we sat in the car for a long moment, no one speaking. Pye had pushed up the bottom of Kelly's dress and was running his hand high over her thigh. She looked frozen. "Smooth," he said. "Really smooth."

"Stop it," I said.

"Go fuck yourself," he said.

I felt the anger rise inside me, and for a moment, I thought I was going to lunge for him, but then I felt Will's gun in my ribs. Will said, "You want to stay friendly. It's best if you do, so I'm really going to heavily suggest it."

Pye said, "Let's all get out."

And so we did. They led us up the rise to where the bulldozer rested, and stopped near it. From where we stood we could peer down into a very large, dark pit behind it. There was enough moonlight I could see that it had been scraped about thirty feet deep and was very wide. In that moment I knew what might end up at the bottom of it. I think it would be nice if I could say I only felt fear for what might happen to Kelly, but the truth was I felt it for myself as well. I had to work to make my knees stay firm and not melt underneath me.

"Lean there against the dozer," Pye told us.

By this time two more men had joined us, came out of nowhere, and suddenly the whole place lit up. There were rows and rows of spotlights on frames, which I had been unaware of on our way up the rise. For a moment I was blinded. The man in front of me was nothing more than a dark shape, then gradually my eyes became reasonably adjusted to the glare, and I was able to get my first real solid look at Pye. As I said, he and his son looked a lot alike, but now that I could see Pye more clearly, I should add that though their resemblance was strong, the elder Anthony's face seemed to hold his past in it, and by that I mean there was something about that face that made me feel even weaker and more lost than I had a moment before. In the dark it was hard, in the light it was a place of ruin. There were bad deeds there, embedded in his flesh like scars; in fact, there were actual scars, and I had seen enough wounds to know that most likely they had come from a knife fight. They stitched little patterns across his cheeks and forehead, like maybe Dr. Frankenstein had put him together in a hurry.

The son came over to stand by him then, and no doubt in my mind when he was his father's age, if he made it that far, they would be twins, minus the knife wounds, unless fate stepped in to help that part out. Right then I would have loved to have been the one to make that possible for the bastard.

"Word—rumor, we'll say—has filtered down to us that you think you saw my son in a car and you think his car hit and killed a woman," said Pye. "Is this true?"

"Yes." Of course, I thought about lying, but I knew that was pointless. If Pye Anthony thought it was really a rumor he wouldn't have bothered to bring us here.

"Ah, okay. Well, rumors like that, they can cause problems. They can cause a man to go to jail, or even be executed, depending on if you can't buy the jury off. Understand?"

"Yes," I said.

"Now, let me put this so you can appreciate it. You and your cunt here need to pay close attention. If you look down into that pit, what I can tell you for sure is people can slip. Right after they get a bullet in their head. Though, like I was saying about your wife, we might have to make sure she gets a bit of entertainment before the bullet—"

"You son of a bitch," I said.

"You are not exactly in a position to be spry, my friend. Kevin."

One of the men, a hulky guy in a black leather coat with a head that looked like at one time might have been in a vice, came forward and slugged me in the stomach, dropping me to my knees. I puked up the nice dinner we had eaten earlier.

"You cowards," Kelly said.

"Would you like to puke too?" Pye said.

I was barely able to say, "Leave it be, Kelly. I'm all right."

I started puking again. No one said anything while I did this.

33

They waited until I was through, almost politely.

When I didn't have anything left inside me to throw up, Kevin grabbed me and pulled me up and shoved me back against the dozer.

"Now, I want you to listen to me," Pye said. "I've been thinking of putting in a pond. Right here. Get some fish, stock it. I have this idea that I could put something in the bottom of this, put a thin film of concrete over it, fill it with water, stock those fish, you know, get a few lily pads and such, and whatever was at the bottom of it all, under the water and the fish and the concrete, no one would ever know about it. You understand what I'm getting at?"

He waited. I realized he really wanted me to answer. I said, "Yes."

"Here's the other thing. I don't have to do that. I should. I could just pop you both and put you down and my troubles with you would be mostly over. But, here's the way I see it. You go missing, and you going to testify and all, well it could come back to me. Most likely will, and then I got to worry with that. It won't change things in the end, but it's got lawyer fees and it's got disruption of business tied to it. So, what I'm going to do is make it real easy for you.… Oh, I almost forgot. Kevin."

Kevin came forward again. He took a cell phone out of his pocket. He pushed Kelly and me together and touched the phone, lighting it up. He tapped the screen. A photo appeared. It was of my mother's house in Manny, Louisiana. He slid his thumb over the screen, bringing up photos of our daughter, Sue. I felt my head swim. Somehow, he knew where she was.

Kevin moved away.

Pye said, "There's always room for one more down there in the bottom of the pit, or two, if we decide your mother would like to join you. I think you're a reasonable man. You want your offspring to survive, your sweet old mother, and this fine wife you have here, so my guess is you're going to decide that you didn't really get that good a look at who was in that car, if in fact you did get a look. You got to thinking you were hasty picking my son out of a mug shot and a lineup, and you just can't say for sure it really was him, and in

34

fact, you're pretty sure it wasn't. I think that's what you're thinking right now. I mean, you know, I'm like a fucking psychic."

He touched his fingers to his head and narrowed his eyes. "Yeah, I'm getting like a goddamn message from beyond, and that message is saying you are going to go home tonight, and be a little restless, but in the morning you are going to go to the police station, and you are going to say just what I told you to say. I got that vision right now, and you know my visions are rarely wrong. And if it should turn out wrong," he said, dropping his hand to his side, "you will be part of my pond, you and your family. You understand that?"

"Yes," I said.

"Say it louder."

"Yes," I said.

"Good. Very good. Now, I was thinking maybe we'd get the phone books, hit you with those awhile, maybe dunk your heads in a vat of water for a bit, just to show we mean business, but it's late, and frankly I'm tired, and I just don't see we need the unpleasantness, which would mostly be about me being up late—and having some things to do early in the morning, that isn't too appealing. That being the case, what I'm going to do is have you get back in the car, and my driver here will take you home, and Kevin will ride with you. Kevin, you can sleep in late in the morning."

Kevin nodded at the news.

"All has been said that needs to be said, I think, so, load up and go home, get a good night's sleep. It's a weekend. Sleep in. Knock you off a piece. Have a nice breakfast. And then, say before noon, go in and talk to the police. Tell them about the error you made. We all of an understanding here, shit crack?"

"We are," I said.

"Good. I like it when we all have the same mind set. Good night, assholes, and remember, you didn't see a goddamn thing. And that includes here. You haven't been here."

Kevin and the driver marched us down to the car and put us in the back. Kevin sat in the front passenger seat, but he was turned so he could look at us. He held a gun in his hand all the while, dangled it over the seat, but not so close I might get hold of it. I watched Kevin while he watched us, him smiling all the while like a shark about to devour us.

They drove us home. The driver got out and opened the door for us like a limousine operator, and left us there on the curb in front of our house.

As soon as they drove away, Kelly burst out crying and I had to support her into the house.

Ten

We waited about thirty minutes, gathering our nerves, going about, trying to figure how they got in the house, and it was pretty easy to determine. They just picked the locks and came inside, easy as picking their nose. There were a few scratches on the carport door lock, but that was it. They had slipped inside, locked the doors back, and waited. I told myself I was going to put locks on all the windows, bars, and that I was going to redo the doors, get some really thick ones, and some out-of-this-world locks that a goddamn safe cracker couldn't pick. I was going to buy a serious alarm system, and a back up to that one. I might get a vicious dog as big as a horse. I thought about all these things, as if it mattered right then. It was like thinking about putting a new barn door on the barn after the mule had run off.

We put on fresh clothes, grabbed a few things, got in our car, and I drove, heading out for Manny, Louisiana, not knowing what else to do, not knowing what to think, but of one thing Kelly was certain.

"You can't testify," she said, as I drove. "You can't. I know you want to do the right thing, but the right thing is taking care of your family. They mean business, baby. Really bad business."

"I know that," I said.

"He may have someone waiting at your mother's house," she said. "He probably will."

"I know that, too."

37

"We have to get Sue."

"I know. And we will."

"If there's someone there—"

"Goddamn it, will you give me a break?"

Kelly shrieked. Just shrieked. Like a banshee. "Don't talk to me like that!"

"I'm sorry. Just … just give me some room. I'm thinking."

"You couldn't do anything tonight, and there's nothing you can do now, no matter how much you think about it. Do you hear me? Nothing."

I had caught a bit of shrapnel over in the sand pit once, being near a friend of mine who caught the bulk of it, killing him, some of it going through his body and striking me, but as horrible as that was, it was nothing compared to what Kelly had said; that wound cut through my soul.

We didn't say much after that, just rode along through the night. We hadn't called ahead, not knowing if we ought to, not knowing why we should. Not knowing much of anything, if you want the truth. All we knew was we were off to get our child and my mother.

After about an hour, Kelly, perhaps in self-defense, fell asleep. What she had said had pained me, made me angry, but that didn't make it any less true. In fact, that's why it had made me so mad. It was true. What the hell could I do? If I didn't testify, Maddy's killer would get away with it. She didn't deserve for that to happen. If I did testify, then my family was in jeopardy. I couldn't let that happen either. I was between a board and nail, and the hammer was cocked and ready to strike.

I thought about all manner of things, and watched the rear-view mirror to try and figure if I was being followed, but nothing struck me as suspicious except for an old pickup truck that was going the same way we were, lagging behind us, but after about twenty minutes it turned off down a side road and I never saw it again.

Then I came back to the thing I was thinking all along, the thing I was trying to avoid. The cell phones Cason had given me and I had put in the glove box of my car.

38

Eleven

When we were near my mother's house, I parked in a church lot about four blocks down from it. I said to Kelly, "If the cops come, tell them you got lost. You know your mother-in-law lives around here somewhere, and you're supposed to pick up your daughter, but you're confused on the house."

"We have a GPS," she said.

"Tell them you're programming it in, then. Tell them you didn't think you needed it, but got this far, realized you did, not having been here in a while." I opened the door and got out, said, "Here, slide over to the driver's side."

"And what if there is someone waiting?"

"I'll cross that bridge when I get to it. There's a whole lot of difference in sneaking up on me while I'm asleep, and me sneaking up on them."

"If you can sneak up on them."

Her lack of confidence wasn't exactly inspiring.

I got out of the car, Kelly slid behind the wheel, and I started walking along the sidewalk on the opposite side of where my mother's house would be. I knew the area as well as I knew my wife's body. I had grown up there. This was a kind of upper scale, suburban area, at least that's what you had to call it compared to most of the town, which was not a metropolis, but a quiet place with people going about their everyday lives, not knowing about people like Pye Anthony and his son, or not wanting to.

I got to thinking as I walked, that if I were one of Pye's guys, I'd be on this side of the street. There were more trees, and the photos I had seen on Kevin's phone had come from the side opposite the house. The guy, or guys that were here to watch the house, could be anywhere, but I got to pondering about how it probably was. I figured for this detail one guy was enough, and for all I knew he had taken the pictures on his phone, sent them, and gone home, thinking that would be enough to have me change my mind. I sure was thinking about changing my mind, so maybe it was enough; almost. I edged past a black Suburban, across a lawn, heard a dog bark, kept going, and fell in under the shadows of some large trees, and then into a brushy trail I had played along as a kid. It had changed some; a few of the trees were gone, and the bushes weren't as wild this time of year, but it was still the same place where I had pretended to be on another planet, waiting any minute for a giant alien insect to strike so I could shoot them down with my trusty ray gun.

I had been certain I was the hero then, and that I would always triumph. After the army, seeing war, I never felt like a hero again. I damn sure didn't feel like one right then.

As I went along, I stooped to pick up a limb that had broken off a tree. It was pretty sturdy and about three feet long. I carried it with me as I walked. When I was close to my mother's house I slowed down and began to watch more carefully. I widened my path, easing through the brush, as the houses disappeared along there, and there was a creek that ran at the end of the street. The creek and a thick clutch of trees made a dead end. Beyond that was another line of trees, then a break and more houses.

Figuring I was overdoing it, but afraid to go straight to the house, I slipped down the slope of the creek and walked along the creek bed, making my way to the side of my mother's home. Before I got there, I decided to climb up the bank and take a peek. I did just that, staying behind a growth of tall grass. I parted it and looked, didn't see anyone. And then that's when it hit me. The black Suburban. It was parked on the street. No other cars were parked on the street. Anyone could do that, park like that, but no one else had. It might mean nothing, and it might mean something. It might mean everything. Like maybe the driver parked a couple blocks up from my mother's house and had walked and found himself a spot where the woods were thick. He could come out of them and take pictures, and he could sit there and wait in case I showed up to get my mother and child and make a break for it. It could be like that. The woods were dense directly across from Mom's house, and certainly to the side of it where the creek ran, which was where I crouched. If someone was there, I figured I had come around behind them past them, and down into the creek.

I remained still for a long moment, watching. I didn't see anyone, but I did see something curious. A little trail of smoke curled out of the woods on my left. It was white and it was snake-like in the moonlight, coiling and uncoiling, and then fading to nothing, followed by yet another snake of smoke, and then another and another.

Me and my large stick eased back down in the creek bed, walked alongside the water, sometimes having to step in it, and I made my way back the way I had come. I climbed out of the creek about where I had gone in, and started back until I found where the trees and bushes were broken apart by a trail. That would be how he had gotten there to the spot where he waited.

I tiptoed down the trail and finally came to where I could see him through a split in the trees where the moonlight fell in. He was sitting in a lawn chair and had a cooler beside the chair. He had a beer on top of the cooler, and lying beside the beer was an automatic pistol.

His position was such that in front of him was a growth of trees and brush. He had a spot to look through, and I could see he had a good view of my mother's house, and even if you were looking for him you couldn't see him. Unless, of course, he was smoking a cigarette, the dumb shit.

I thought about what I would set in motion if I did what I was thinking about doing, but I didn't consider it for very long. As I said, I thought about many things, but at the bottom of it all I knew what I was going to do. I was going to testify, and I wasn't going to let anything or anyone get in my path and stop me.

Slipping along quietly, I raised the limb over my shoulder, and just as I was on him I guess he heard me, because his hand reached out slowly for his gun, like maybe he was being foolish, thinking perhaps it was just a possum in the brush. But this possum was armed with a limb. As his head turned slightly, I swung it. I swung for the fences. Baby Ruth never made a swing so good. I caught him up side the head so hard I knocked him out of the lawn chair, sending his cigarette spinning, spilling him out on the ground, and then I went to work. He tried to get up, but I hit him under the ear with the limb, and when he ducked his head, I cut down on him right where the back of the head sloped. It was a good lick. He went down and lay still. I hit him again for good measure. He still didn't move.

I bent down and touched his neck. He was alive. I thought about killing him, I won't kid you, but that wasn't something I could do. Not even under these circumstances. At least not yet. Not if I could avoid it.

Dropping the limb, I got his gun and checked the action, slipped it in my pants pocket. It didn't quite fit, but the pants were loose, so it served as a kind of holster. I flipped the lid open on the cooler, causing his beer to fly off. Inside was a bit of crushed ice floating in water, and there were three beers. I took one out and opened it and drank it almost in one giant slurp. I crushed the can and tossed it in the watery cooler and closed the lid, pushed my way through the brush and started across the street to my mother's house, pausing by the creek long enough to toss the gun through the brush there and into the water, listening to its satisfying splash.

42

Twelve

It was late and I knocked gently on the door, but didn't rouse Mom. I had to go around to the bedroom window and knock, finally got her up. She pulled back the curtains and stared out at me. Her graying hair was a little wild, and she had the look she had when I was a kid and she caught me doing something stupid.

When she raised the window, she said, "What are you doing here, son?"

"Mom, this is going to sound crazy, but we have to get Sue, and we have to go."

"Go? Now? Tonight?"

"I said it would sound crazy, didn't I? And it is, a little, but trust me, we have to go."

She stared at me a moment, blinking sleep out of her eyes, holding her nightgown at her throat as if it might escape.

"I can explain on the way. Get a few things for yourself, grab Sue's stuff, and we'll go."

"Go where?"

"We'll cross that bridge when we come to it. I'll meet you at the front door in fifteen minutes."

"Son, I don't understand."

"Do you trust me?"

"Of course."

"Then get the stuff and meet me at the door in fifteen minutes. No more questions right now."

I walked back to where the man lay and looked down at him. He was still out. I bent and got his shoestrings out of his shoes and pulled his hands behind his back and tied them together with one lace, tied his ankles together with the other. In time he'd work himself loose, or maybe if he was strong enough, break the shoestrings. But it might give us a little leverage to have him tied for a while.

Finished with him, I walked back to the church lot.

"What took so long?" Kelly said, as I was sliding in on the passenger's side.

"There was someone watching."

"Oh my god."

"He's taken care of."

"You killed him?"

"No. But I gave him a headache. Come on, hurry. Drive to the house."

I was hoping for a bit of respect with that comment, but was uncertain if I got any.

Kelly drove us to Mom's house and I got out and knocked gently on the door. Mom had dressed in jeans and a loose shirt, and she came out carrying Sue who was still in her nightgown and mostly asleep; she looked like a little black-haired doll slung over my mother's shoulder. I felt a rush of emotion rise up in me so fast and hot, for a moment I thought I might throw up.

I got myself together, took the single bag by the door, and put it in the trunk of the car, and Kelly drove us away.

Thirteen

We drove out of Manny, started back in the direction of home, though I didn't have plans to go back there tonight. Sue came awake long enough to speak to us, but then she was out like a light, lying in the backseat with her head in Mom's lap. I told Mom all that happened.

"Oh my god," she said.

"We're going to have to stash you with Sue somewhere until we can get this straightened out."

"He can straighten it out by not testifying," Kelly said.

"No, he can't," Mom said. "He's got to do what's right."

"Taking care of the family, that's what's right," Kelly said.

"And what kind of family is it that lets a killer go free?" Mom said.

"So he puts him in jail and we all die?" Kelly said. "How's that work out in anybody's favor? That sound right to you?"

"Of course not," Mom said. "But you don't quit on something like this just because it's hard. And I'll tell you whose favor it works out in, this Anthony character. It isn't easy, but you don't quit."

"We could quit," Kelly said.

"Yes," Mom said. "You could. But should you?"

I tried to ease the tension. "I've got an idea. Something that I kind of set up earlier."

"Oh, good," Kelly said.

"That didn't sound too sincere," I said.

45

"You think?"

I had gone from the most wonderful person in her life to a toad overnight, and just because I had witnessed a crime. Knocking that thug in the head hadn't earned me any points.

I opened the glove box and took out one of the burner phones. I called Cason.

After he got himself awake, he said, "I figure you're calling me on this phone you've made a decision to do something other than leave your protection to the law."

"It may be worse than just having protection," I said, and I told him all that had happened.

"Shit," he said. "That has gone south. All right, I'm going to call you back, and it's okay to keep this phone for a bit, but after I call you back, get rid of it. How's everyone doing?"

"Scared. Like me."

"Good. You should be. You'll last longer that way. Booger is the only person in the world who can be foolishly brave and survive. The devil doesn't want him, and I don't blame the old son-of-a-bitch."

I cut the connection and we cruised for another fifteen minutes, sitting in silence, and then Kelly said to my mom, "I'm sorry, Evelyn."

"No problem. Good families know how to quarrel. I used to have it out with Tom's dad. He'd get so mad he'd speak Chinese to me. When we got to that point, I knew I had to let him cool off, so I'd at least know what he was saying."

"No. I mean you're right," Kelly said. "You both are. Tom, who were you talking to?"

I explained about Cason, told them a little about Booger.

"Can they help us?"

"The real answer is I don't know. But I think so. It's not like we've got a lot of options. I been thinking. How did Pye know where my mom was, that Sue was with her?"

"Guess it's not that hard to find out," Kelly said.

"But who did we tell? Or rather, who did I tell that I had seen

46

Will Anthony?"

"The police," Kelly said. "No one else."

"Exactly."

"Oh, hell," Kelly said. "You mean ..."

"I think so. Remember how they were telling us that I didn't have to put myself on the spot, almost like they were trying to convince me to stay silent."

"It could have been that, I guess," Kelly said. "They could have just been being honest."

"Maybe," I said.

The cell phone rang.

I put it to my ear, said, "Yes."

"I got a place you can go. It's in Arkansas. A buddy of Booger's. No one's there, but you can use it. You got to drive out in the country a bit. It'll be a long night."

"Not like we have a lot of choices."

"You have a GPS?"

"Yes."

He gave me the directions and I typed them in. It was one of those GPS devices that didn't work when the car was moving, so we had to pull over to the side of the road while I did the work. Cason said that would get me close, then he'd have to give me the rest of the directions from there; it wouldn't be on the GPS, too out in the boonies.

"You go there, sleep, and then come back home tomorrow by yourself," he said. "Leave your family there. There will be a car for them; a pickup, actually. Also, the house is stocked with basic food, and the water works and so does the electricity. There's no phone. It's best your family doesn't go anywhere. It's unlikely those assholes can find the place, but it's best if they stay out of sight."

"All right," I said.

"You come back tomorrow, go to the police and tell them about the threat. Get it on record. I don't care what they told you, you do that."

"I think the cops might be involved. I told you that."

"Could be," he said. "But if they know you aren't afraid of the guy, that you're going to put him on record, then that actually makes the case against the kid stronger."

"It's all hearsay," I said.

"Yeah, but you still want it on record."

"It is on record," I said.

"Yeah, but this way you find out what they plan to do a whole lot quicker. If the cops are in on it, we push them to make a move, and we'll be waiting."

"I feel like I'm walking into the lion's jaws."

"You're showing the lion you're not afraid of it."

"But I am. Didn't you say it was good to be scared?"

"Did I? Yeah, I probably did. Sounds like me. You know what, that's still good advice. But you should go to the cops for the reason I said. It makes it a little harder for whoever there is spilling to Anthony to make things hard for you without exposing themselves."

"What if it's not just one cop, and they're all on the take?"

"That would be a major problem," he said. "I think we'd all be fucked. But I got a little more faith in the law than that; just not a whole lot more."

"Great," I said.

Fourteen

The cabin was in the deep Arkansas woods, and it was late morning when we got there. It was pretty big. A white pickup was parked out front. It was old but had good tires, and according to Cason it ran just fine. The cabin had seen better days as well, but the roof was sturdy, the walls were made of treated logs, and the keys for the cabin and truck were hidden where Cason said they would be.

We were all exhausted. There were two small bedrooms. Kelly and I took one, Mom and Sue the other. As soon as my head hit the pillow I was out like a light.

I woke up about eleven the next morning and was grateful Sue kept sleeping well into the day. I didn't want to try and explain anything to her. I kept slipping into the room where she and Mom were, looking at her, assuring myself she was all right. I had dreamed about her being taken out of the window at night, taken out of there by Pye Anthony and his son Will. It was a horrible dream, but I was so deep down into it I couldn't wake myself up, couldn't get up to check on Sue, and now I was doing it in broad daylight without any reason to do so, other than self-satisfaction.

Kelly slept on as well. And that was good. I needed time to myself, to collect my thoughts and sort them, if that was possible.

About noon I started some coffee, and then I went outside and broke up the burner phone on a brick cooking grill. I broke it and then stepped on it and tossed it away. I should have done it last night, though I didn't know who it was that would be interested in tracking me, or even if they could.

Back inside the house, I saw the coffee was ready, and about then Kelly drifted in rubbing her eyes. We had only brought a few things with us, and one of those was one of my old tee-shirts, and she was wearing it as a nightgown. It almost hung to her knees.

"Coffee?" I said.

"Sure."

"I looked around," I said. "They got some instant oatmeal, granola bars, nothing fresh. Breakfast or lunch is pretty much the same thing."

"Granola bar will be fine."

I got us both a granola bar and a cup of coffee. We sat at the kitchen table.

"I love you," Kelly said, "and I know I apologized last night, but I go from one moment to the other about what to do, so please don't think I'm blaming you."

"It's all right."

It wasn't, but it was something to say.

I poured her a cup of coffee. "No milk or sugar," I said.

"I need it straight and leaded," she said. She sipped a little of it, said, "What's this plan you were talking about?"

"It might be best you don't know," I said.

"It involves you getting hurt, I'm against it."

"I can't promise one way or another about that," I said. "That thing Pye Anthony said, last night, about how he and his bunch would leave us alone if we didn't testify. Okay, maybe he meant for the time being. But say I don't testify. His boy gets off, goes scot-free. We got to think they might decide they don't want the situation to come up again, and when things calm down, they might arrange for us to have an accident, or disappear."

"I didn't think about that."

"Makes sense, doesn't it?"

She nodded.

"I don't want us looking over our shoulders the rest of our lives, and we have Sue to think about. When she gets older, she wants

50

to play soccer, baseball, go on a band trip, we got to wonder who's watching her, waiting for her to be alone, to punish us just for me thinking about testifying. Lieutenant Ernest said they lived by the feud, that they were petty. They could wait quite a while before exacting revenge."

"So you're thinking there is no safety net?"

"Not the way Pye's laying it out."

"So what's the answer?"

"I think: what would my father have done? What would have been his approach?"

"And what did you decide he would have done?" she asked.

"He'd testify."

"And what about his family?"

"He would have made sure they were safe. Whatever it took. He was old-school on that matter. Law-abiding American citizen, but if you decided to bypass the law, I think he would have made the same choice. He'd have put their asses down and told god they fell off a bicycle."

"Look, I get it," she said. "You want to protect your family at all costs, but if you go to prison doing it, that won't help us any. And killing. Can you do that?"

"I have," I said.

"That was the war," she said.

"This is war. But don't misunderstand me. That's the last thing I want to do, that I want to happen. And if the cops are in on it, well … It's like I said, baby. I don't want to spend every night in a cold sweat, every trip to town looking in my rear-view mirror. There's some guys I know from the sand pit that maybe can help me."

"The Army?"

I nodded.

"This Cason fellow?" she asked.

"Yes. And someone far less nice."

"I don't like the sound of that."

"It's not about how it sounds," I said. "It's about not dying."

I stayed in the cabin until Sue and Mom woke up. Sue and I went out and walked down to the creek on the property. We watched minnows swim in a shallow part of it. We tossed some rocks together and talked about silly stuff. When we walked back to the cabin an hour or so later, me holding her little hand, I told her I loved her and how I had to go back on business, but how she would be fine with Mom and Grandma. I went inside and joined my mother and Kelly. They were staring at me anxiously.

I gave Kelly the keys to the truck, most of the money from my wallet. "Don't use your credit cards, in case these guys can trace them."

"How would they do that?"

"If they are in cahoots with the police, that's how. Computers. They can link up and find out about anything. Shit, Kelly, I don't know. But don't do it. Cason seems to know about these things, and he wants us to stay away from telephones, land lines, or our cells. I trust him."

"All right," she said. "Not that there are any phones here, except my cell."

"Don't use it," I said.

"I won't," Kelly said. "I promise."

"The money," I said, "you shouldn't need it for anything, but if there's a worst-case scenario, and you have to leave, you might need to put more gas in the truck. Cason said it was full."

"What about the person who owns the cabin?" Mom asked.

"No worries," I said. "Cason has worked that out. He won't be coming back for a while. He owes Booger a favor, and if you owe him one, you want to do what you can to clear that ledger as quick as possible."

Mom said, "You do what you have to do, son. I know you will. We'll be fine."

Kelly walked me out to our car. I said, "You may not have the best of provisions, but you've got food. Cason said the TV works, but there's only DVDs. I hope you like action movies. I looked through them this morning. In this cabin Burt Reynolds is still king. I'll get back in touch with you. If I don't, a guy named Cason Statler will, or another guy named Booger. Or that friend of Booger's who owns this cabin."

"Booger? First name or last name?"

"Booger is good enough."

I took her in my arms. She said, "I hate being such a scaredy cat."

"You take care of our baby," I said. "You take care of her and tell her I love her."

"What if we're here when school starts?"

"You won't be," I said. I didn't mention to her that I assumed if she was, I wouldn't be coming home.

We kissed for a long time. It was a good kiss. Not a sexual kiss, not a husband-and-wife peck on the lips. It was a possible kiss goodbye. There was a lot of apology in it, on both sides.

By the time I had driven out of the woods and hit a major highway, it was late afternoon, near dark. I took the second burner phone out of the glove box.

I called Cason. "I'm on my way back to Laborde."

"All right, here's what you do," he said. "You meet me and Booger at my place."

He gave me the address in Camp Rapture. I pulled over and tapped it in the GPS, then, leaving the motor running, I got out and put the phone under the front wheel of the car and drove over it and went on, trying desperately not to drive too fast, thinking about what it was I was going to do, what Cason and Booger were going to do. I thought about my family. I thought about our home. I thought about those weasels, breaking into our house, taking us out to that goddamn pit in the middle of the night and threatening our lives. I thought about what Cason had told me they had done to that man, cutting off his legs, and later coming back to finish him off, making home plate out of him, having his hand glued to his dick. I thought about all that so much, I'd find my foot shoving down hard on the gas. I finally set the cruise control and tried to keep my foot off the pedal.

When I left Afghanistan I wanted to be through with violence. I believed it was the law's job in a civilized world, but what if there was no law, and what if the world wasn't all that civilized? What if you couldn't trust the law? What if the law was on the side of those who were trying to harm you? What then? What was the answer?

Fifteen

It was pretty late when I got back to East Texas; early morning, actually, but still solid dark. I drove through Laborde, past my frame shop, kept on driving toward Camp Rapture.

I drove to the address Cason had given me. He had a large apartment down on Main Street. It was above a sandwich shop next to a yoga studio. I coasted around back, the way he had told me. There was an alley, and off the alley was a driveway, and there was a bright light on a pole and it was easy to see how to go. I parked behind a big black truck that was so high off the ground it looked like you needed a hot-air balloon to get up to the door. In front of it was an elderly white car, a Ford. It looked like it had seen better days. There was another car there too, an old Volkswagen Beetle.

When I was parked, Booger came out. He had been waiting on me. He was just the way I remembered him. Like Cason, he didn't appear to have aged a bit. He had the kind of look that made you wonder what his ethnicity was. Black maybe, though more the color of coffee splashed with milk. Hispanic? A bit of Asian, like me? What he was mostly was broad-shouldered, shaved head, and all muscle. He was handsome in a stone-cold-killer kind of way. He had all the right features, but there was something off about him. Back in the sand pit I thought maybe it was his nose that was not being quite right, or his eyes not being even. But it wasn't any of that. All of that fit okay if you studied him hard enough. It was something about the way he looked at you, about the way he smiled.

How his lips and eyes moved, but the flesh on his face didn't move all that much. He was like a living, walking, breathing, bloodthirsty automaton.

"Hey, Tom, you old goat-fucker. How you been?"

"Not that good."

"Oh, yeah. Well, I knew that. Force of habit, asking like that, like maybe I really give a shit."

He stuck out his hand and we shook. He tried to crush my paw just like in the old days.

When he let go of my hand he put his arm around my shoulders and started walking me toward the stairs that led up to the top apartment. "Heard you drive up, buddy. Cason is in the shower. We got a beer in here with your name on it, if you want it."

"Sure, Booger. Thanks for helping me out, man."

"Oh, shit, Tom. Don't flatter yourself. I don't give a flying shit about you really. You know that."

"I do?"

"I'm doing this for Cason. Hell, he wanted me to kill you, right now, I would. And there's another reason I'm doing it."

We were up the stairs and going inside by this time. He removed his arm from my shoulders. He looked at me and his mouth opened in a thin smile, his eyes were as cold as if he were dead and the morning frost were resting on them. "I like killing."

On that note he slapped me on the shoulder, motioned me toward the couch, and got me a beer. I sat there nervously, wondering if he might get bored and go off his nut and murder me for entertainment. I wasn't any pushover when I had the chance, but Booger? Well, he wasn't entirely human.

He sat in a chair and looked at me. It was a strange look, like a snake studying the rat it was about to bite. "You're the same as you were over there," he said.

"Yeah," I said. "And how is that?"

"You don't like the work."

"No," I said. "If you mean killing. No. I don't like the work."

"I'd still be killing those bastards over there, any bastards, I don't

56

give a damn. I'd be killing them, I wasn't put out of the service. They said they wanted people dead, but they didn't want them as dead as I did."

"I think they had certain people in mind under certain circumstances," I said. "Not just anyone."

"And therein lay the problem," he said. "What you got to understand is we're put here to compete with one another, to make room for ourselves. It's all just one big fucking rat-fuck game, partner. It's a game played during a storm, and all you can do is play it out until the storm blows your ass away."

Cason came into the room then. He was wearing gray sweatpants and rubbing his damp hair with a towel. He was one of those guys who actually spent a lot of time at the gym, had that six-pack. That gave me another reason to envy him. Good looks and the will to keep his body in tip-top shape. I had a hard time walking on my treadmill three times a week.

"Hey, Tom," he said.

"Hey," I said.

"You giving him the 'life is a chaotic game in the midst of a storm' speech?" Cason asked Booger.

"You bet," Booger said. "I was just about to wax poetic on it, and in you came, fucking it up."

Cason said, "Let's get right down to it. I want you to tell me everything that happened again, all the details, in case you left something out. Be thorough. It might be important. When you finish, you nap out here awhile; daylight gets solid, you go to the cops, like I told you. Let's see how you stand with them, see what they're really about, if we can. It's nice to know how many players are actually on the field."

I told him everything, more specific than before. I even mentioned that Kelly and I had been nude and had to dress in front of them. Just telling them that humiliated me all over again. Booger seemed to be enjoying the story. He probably didn't understand the humiliation part.

When I finished, Cason said, "Here's how it is. I've been

dealing with these kinds of assholes as a reporter for years. I've been threatened, and a couple of times I was on a hit list, but the way these guys operate, the ones we're talking about, it's not like there's a true chain of command. It's one or two guys that are running things, and everyone else works for them. They're loyal as long as the paychecks come in. We get the old man, and send the kid downtown to the concrete box, or kill him too, then it's over for you. The old man has the power and the money, not the kid. I'm not saying that Pye's guys won't make that hard for us to do, getting those two, but I am saying once they're out of the picture, so are their worker's paychecks. Maybe there's some guy left that takes over, but it's not in his best interest to pursue you, and in fact, with the two Anthonys out of the picture, the new guy has a shot at the organization, they'll try and take over, and the hell with the Anthonys."

"Then maybe we don't have to get too dirty," I said, "if we just nip those two."

"Oh, we'll get dirty all right."

I didn't really want to remind Cason of the obvious, but I said it anyway. "You don't have to do this, you know. I don't want to pull you into something that might get you in deep shit. I mean, we're old army buddies, you and I, but still."

"This guy, Pye, he's like the one before him, and the one that'll be after him. They're all the same. They think they own the goddamn world, and the problem is they do own a piece of it, and part of that piece is a lot of the bad stuff that goes on in my hometown and yours, all of East Texas. Guys like that, they got to be stepped on, and when a new one steps up, someone has to step on them, same as cockroaches."

"I'm all for stepping on cockroaches," I said. "But for me, it's less noble than that. It's about me and my family. That's my mission."

Booger said, "Point me at who you want done, and it's done, and I don't give a shit about cockroaches or family."

"We'll have to do a little more planning," Cason said. "But basically, they're coming for you, Tom. The cops, if someone there is in on it, we can't count on them. But even if we were counting on them, they only have so many men and so many police hours to offer. We'll start out just being your emergency backup and hope we don't need more than that, though that's highly unlikely. Booger here has a bodyguard agency, and he'll be there to protect you in a semi-legal way, depending on what we end up doing and what they find out, which if we're lucky, will be very little."

"Yep," Booger said. "And I'm the only bodyguard in the agency."

"That's right," Cason said. "But you write him out a check. You've hired him. He has the right to be there to protect you as long as he doesn't break any laws. That they know about."

"I got a fucking license and everything," Booger said. "But I'll tell you, it would be simpler just to hunt them down, bring a few party favors, and get it done, kill every man jack of them."

"I'd rather just try and be protected," I said.

"Oh, don't misunderstand me," Cason said. "That's our pose if they find out Booger is there. In the long run protection itself won't work."

"Then what are you talking about?" I said.

"Long as either of the Anthonys can get to you, or can pay someone on the outside to get to you, you aren't safe. I'm saying we're going to make it look like a bodyguard job. In the end, I figure we'll end up doing something like Booger has suggested, because that's about the only alternative there really is."

"So we're going to kill them?" I said.

"You aren't really that dull," Booger said. "What do you think we're talking about, giving them a hand job? Yeah, we're going to kill them. So dead. So damn dead."

Sixteen

Of course I knew that, and had been thinking it myself, and had even suggested as much to Kelly, but I needed to hear them say it, I guess. Still, I didn't like the idea. Not even a little bit. You don't forget dead bodies. It's not like in the movies, like someone lying down to sleep. It's nothing like that. There is something so strange and cold about it, and not like a dead person in a coffin either. Much more pathetic, and made all the worse by bloody wounds. And there's the smell of blood and intestines, and finally, if the bodies have lain there for a while, the smell of decomposition. That smell you never forget. That stink stays in your nose forever. Sometimes in a dream I'll see the bodies I saw in Afghanistan, sometimes Afghans, sometimes American soldiers, and I swear, I can smell that fresh bloody stench of death, and then I can smell that other stink, the one that comes from decay, and I'll wake up, sit up in bed, and the stink is still with me. So strong I have to get up and go downstairs and wait until it passes, letting time act like a breeze that blows it away.

I was thinking about all this as I drove to the police station that morning. I hadn't slept much, a couple of hours, and then I was up making coffee. Booger was up too. He didn't seem to have slept or needed it. I got out of there as soon as I could. Booger made me nervous.

When I got to the station, I went past the bald cop again, who lifted his hand to wave this time. I easily found Lieutenant Ernest. He was in his office pushing some papers around on his desk top.

The door was open and I went in and sat in the chair in front of his desk. He smiled at me.

"You look a little haggard, Tom."

"You have an idea why, I presume."

"Yeah, I do. It would make anyone nervous."

"I want you to know that I've put my family someplace safe, so it's just me you got worry about."

"Where did you put them?"

"I'm going to keep that to myself. I figure if no one knows but me, then it's a safer place."

"You can tell me."

"But I won't."

"Tom, I'm the police. I should probably know."

"They're safe," I said. "That's good enough."

"All right. Have it your way."

"There's me, though. I could use some protection."

"We can do that. You're still going to testify?"

"You act like you think there might be a reason I wouldn't."

"No more than what I told you before," he said.

"When's the trial?" I asked.

He leaned back in his chair. "That I can't say. That's up to the judge. Will Anthony already has a lawyer."

"So he knows I'm going to testify?" I said.

"He has a lawyer on retainer when he needs her," Ernest said. "He doesn't know he needs her yet. No one's told him. I'm just saying, he has a lawyer and he'll go straight to her soon as he knows about you."

"Look here, I said, "I may hire a bodyguard."

"A bodyguard?"

"It's just a thought," I said. "I haven't put it in concrete."

"I can put someone on it, park near your house in an unmarked car."

"Near my house?" I said. "And what if they come in the back door, or for that matter through the front while your man is snoozing?"

"He won't be snoozing. That's insulting."

"You can get over an insult; I might not get over a bullet," I said.

He didn't like that, and I could see what he didn't like moving around on his face, but after a while his features calmed. "I see your point. I can recommend someone if you want to go that route."

"I have an old army buddy that runs a service like that," I said. "I'll go to him, I figure."

"You won't need it,' he said. "We can do the job."

"What if Will's not convicted," I said. "You going to keep watching after me?"

"I've warned you about the problems with testifying," he said. "No. We won't be able to do that after the trial. Those are things to think about for sure."

I stood up. "When does your policeman start?"

"Since Will doesn't know we have you, or what you know, you're not in any danger at the moment, so when the trial is set would be good. When Will's lawyer knows about you, for certain."

"All right, then."

I turned and started out the door.

"Tom," he said.

I turned back to him. He said, "What you're doing is brave. I want to tell you that. I thank you. The city thanks you. The state thanks you. But, it could be a foolish decision."

"You keep saying that," I said, and left out of there.

When I was down the road a bit, I took one of the two new burner phones Cason had given me that morning, and called him.

"Yes," he said.

"Kind of like you and I figured," I said. "Lieutenant Ernest. He's in on it."

"You know that for a fact?" Cason asked.

"No, but I think he's in on it."

"That's not quite the same thing," he said.

"Bottom line, I don't trust him. I didn't trust him to begin with, but now I really don't trust him. I can't say I know anything more than I knew before, but I'm going to play it like he's in on it. That seems the safe way."

"I'm going to agree with you," he said. "I thought he might slip up in such a way you'd know something solid, but even if you don't, we got to assume he's in with Anthony, for caution's sake. What are you doing right now?"

"Frankly, I don't know."

"Come see me again."

Seventeen

I drove over to Cason's, and it was a pretty good drive, of course, all the way to Camp Rapture. When I was inside his place, he held out his hand. There was a .38 revolver in it. He said, "Here's a nice and simple pistol Booger left you."

"How sweet of him," I said.

"It's clean," he said. "You have your own gun?"

"I'm not a real fan of guns," I said. "After the war I'm less of one, but yeah, I have a shotgun."

"Someone breaks in, use it, not this," he said, referring to the revolver. "I mean, you got to, it's what's there, go ahead and we'll cross that bridge when we come to it, but you'd have a hard time explaining killing an intruder with a clean gun. The shotgun, that's yours. This one, it's for work outside the home, so to speak."

"Where's Booger?" I took the revolver.

"He's at your house. I dropped him off there a while back. Or close enough."

"What if he was seen?" I said. "Someone may already be watching."

"He wasn't seen. You can count on that. Not in any way anyone would understand it was him. He's like a goddamn ghost when he wants to be. You should remember that from the old days."

"Yeah, I guess I should. I don't like him."

"I don't know if you should," Cason said. "I worry about me because I do. Kind of. Truth is, I try to stay away from him normally.

65

He's a big accident waiting to happen."

"Hope this isn't the accident," I said.

"He's what I've got," Cason said. "He's what you've got. What you do is you go home. Be cautious, but know Booger is in the house. I doubt anyone that might have showed up got past him, and if they did, they didn't get completely past him. You'll find someone dead, even if he's amongst them."

"Comforting."

"You go inside and wait until we make our next move, which is simple. We go after them."

"And when will that be?" I asked.

"Maybe tonight, maybe tomorrow night. I'm going to come take Booger's place, just a friend coming to visit. At that point Booger is going to slip out and do a bit of reconnaissance. We'll wait to hear what he says before we have a war council. I also have a place in Laborde I've rented. A little pool house out back of a friend's house. Now and again I go there to pretend I'm working on my book, or because I have a reporter story out of Laborde. So I'll be close by."

I drove home then. Knowing Booger was supposed to be in the house didn't curb my fears. I had the .38 revolver in my glove box, and as I pulled into the carport I took it out, held it by my side as I unlocked the door.

Easing inside, the gun held before me, I said, "Booger?"

There wasn't any answer. I looked through the house. He was nowhere to be seen. I padded silently into the bedroom. A cold snake of fear slithered up by back. I turned and the pistol was snatched from my hand and the next thing I knew I was on the floor on my back and there was a gun stuck against my forehead.

The gun went away, and a face, like a comet falling, dropped down close to mine. "You got to get your juice back, Tom, my man. And don't call my name, even if you think I'm here. Someone else might be here, and I might be hiding to tag them."

Booger stood, held out a hand and helped me up. He was wearing a cap and gray work clothes that had the name of the local cable company stenciled on both.

66

"Damn, Booger. You scared me to death."

"I know."

"Where the fuck were you?"

"Right by you most of the time. I'm in your house, Tom, and you didn't even notice me."

"You're like some fucking ninja."

"Yes, I am. But I'm a hungry ninja. Can you fix something to eat?"

I went in and whipped us up a couple of large omelets, got a pot of coffee going. We were in the kitchen, and at the back of the house is a double-wide glass door. The curtains were drawn over it. While I cooked Booger stood at the corner of the curtains, peeking out now and again. He said, "I figure they come, they'll come through here or the carport. If they come through the front door, it'll be under some ruse. The latches are easy to jimmy on all the doors, the carport especially. Cason dropped me off a block up. I walked over, stopping to look around like I was doing something important, carrying a clipboard. I got here, I walked into the carport like I owned it, and when I was sure no one was looking, I went through the gate into the backyard, jimmied this door, and I was in. Saw a photo of your wife in your office, by the way. She's a hot piece of ass."

"I prefer you not call my wife a piece of ass," I said.

"That was a compliment," he said.

"I know, but it's an uncomfortable one," I said.

He nodded. "All right. Whatever you say. You know, I was wondering. Are you part Asian?"

"Of course I am. You've known me for this long, and you didn't know that. My last name is Chan. That's not Polish."

"All right, I knew. I just wanted to ask."

"Yeah. Asian. My dad was born in Hong Kong. He became an American citizen when he was a child. I'm also Irish. My mother is so Irish she spits shamrocks."

"Yeah, you look a little like a blue-eyed Chinaman. I just couldn't decide if your eyes squinted enough. Mine don't squint much, and

I've got some chink in me, some nigger, some Jew, you name it. It's all the same. All people, whatever they are, what mix they are, bleed, and I bleed. But mostly, if I'm involved, they bleed."

He grinned at me like I was supposed to have gotten some kind of joke.

I put the food on plates and got out silverware, wondering if I was more frightened of Booger than I was of Pye and Will Anthony.

We sat around like that for a while, Booger prattling on about this and that, telling me about all the women he'd had and how anal was the best if they were greased up right. I was a nervous wreck by the time it grew dark, and when the door buzzer rang I nearly jumped three feet.

Booger said, "Wait here."

He made for the door, quiet as a mouse in moccasins. I had the thirty-eight in my hand by that time, forgetting what Cason had told me about the shotgun. Booger peeked out the spy hole, turned his head to me, said, "Cason."

He opened the door and let him in.

Eighteen

Booger had a bag in the closet, took it out and put on black clothes, stuck a black ski mask in his pants pocket. I realized Cason, except for the hood, was dressed the same way. Cason was wearing a cap, similar to the one Booger had been wearing, but without the logo. Not that anyone could see the logo at night.

I got it then. Booger was going to walk out and drive away in Cason's car. Just a friend who came to visit for a while, then left. Anyone was watching, they probably wouldn't think much of it. Fact was they'd wait to get me alone if they could. Seeing Booger leave might excite them to action.

Before Booger left, we all had a cup of coffee so it wouldn't seem like too short a visit, then Booger said, "Now it's time to go amongst them."

Booger adjusted his cap, pulling it down low, took a couple of handguns from the bag and stuck them under his shirt and went out without another word. I went to the spy hole and could see him get in the car at the curb and drive away.

"He looks too big to be you," I said.

"I doubt they'll notice that," Cason said. "They saw me come in, and they expect to see me go out, and that's what they'll see. It's kind of like a magic trick. The magician makes you see what he wants you to see, not what you're really looking for. That's of course if there's anyone out there to see anything."

We sat around for a while, and though Cason was pretty solid, he was more nervous than Booger. Now and again, sitting there at the table, he'd smile at me to let me know he knew how I felt. We didn't talk, or go into the living room to watch television. We didn't play chess or cards. We didn't do anything to distract us. I hid the .38, got the shotgun out of the bedroom closet and got the shells out of the shoebox up on the top shelf of the closet, and loaded it. I kept the shotgun and shells separated because of Sue. I had inherited the shotgun from my father, who was something of an East Texas-Chinese redneck, and I kept it for protection from a common burglar or a poisonous snake in the yard. I knew how to use it, but I still didn't like it, not after my time in the war.

As it got near ten o'clock, we cut off the light in the kitchen and moved to the hall. We sat down in the hallway, our backs against the wall, facing one another in the dark. We were at the edge where the kitchen began, and by leaning a little to the side, I could see the door to the carport. The hallway led to the front door and all we had to do was turn our heads to see it, maybe twenty feet from us. Look to the right and we could see the sliding back doors. We had all the doors covered, if not the windows. I, of course, worried about the windows. Hell, I worried about the doors. I worried about them coming through the ceiling. I worried.

I said, "You're not a bodyguard. What if they come and you're here, and you have to shoot someone? How do we explain that?"

"I'm your friend. I have a concealed-carry license. I carry it because I've written some articles that have made some bad people mad. I had my gun with me. We heard a noise. You got your shotgun. I drew my nine, and there we have it. That's as good as it gets, and if we stick to that, we're all right. I think."

"You think?"

"Yep. I think."

We sat there for a long time, and finally I got up and made fresh coffee and we had a cup, sitting in the hallway with it, and when we finished I put the cups away and came back and sat down. The minutes went by like old, crippled convicts in chains.

Coffee and adrenaline kept me wired and awake, and I guess

that's why my stomach was queasy as well. That and fear and confusion and wondering how the hell I had ever come to this, part of me thinking if I hadn't looked around the corner of the house right when I did, had I been a bit slower, I wouldn't be carrying all this concern and the fear. But I had. There was no way to reverse that. I could do like Kelly had wanted me to do and bail, but I would think about that every day of my life, and even then I wouldn't be safe; my family wouldn't be safe. There was no other course, good or bad, than the one I was on. It was like I was on a train and knew at the end of the tracks was a cliff and there was no other choice but to go over it, no way off that train.

That's when Booger said, "I took a look."

He was standing right at the edge of the hallway, on the carport side. His pants were dirty and a little damp, his shoes were dripping mud.

Cason said, "Goddamn, Booger, I nearly shit my pants."

"If I had been them other guys, you'd have bled your pants as well," he said.

"They couldn't sneak up on me like that," Cason said.

"You say," Booger said.

"Did you come through the carport?" I asked.

"Yep."

"I just looked that way," I said.

"Not when I was coming through."

"We could have shot you," I said.

"No. Don't think so."

"Why didn't you come through the front door, they're watching, they would see you come back and think you're still me," Cason said.

"Oh, I parked out front and walked into the carport casual like," Booger said. "I didn't care if they saw me. They'd just think I was the same guy, and I was using the carport door. But, you know what? No one is out there. Not yet. The cops say they don't need to be here because no one knows, and Pye Anthony, he can set his own time. Besides, I just wanted to see the look on your faces when

71

I snuck up on you."

"Yeah," Cason said, "quite the fucking joke."

"Look, let's sit at the table," Booger said. "It's nearly daylight and I'm so hungry I could peck corn out of hog shit and eat it."

"I was a little hungry," I said. "Not so much now."

Nineteen

I got down some bowls, cereal and milk, tossed some turkey bacon in a pan, and set it to frying. I poured out the old coffee and started some new. I put toast in the toaster. Cason and Booger sat at the table. A long blade of light was sneaking in through the corners of the curtains over the sliding glass door to the backyard.

"I went out to where you told me they took you and your wife," Booger said. "I parked down the road a piece, on a little logging trail, got out and made my way through the woods, came to a rise in the trees that overlooked the construction site. One thing you can be certain, there's a bunch of them."

Booger was pouring cereal in his bowl, measuring it out carefully. "I got a pretty good look at some of them. I thought about killing them right then, but I didn't know exactly how many were there and though there were guns in the car, right with me I just had the two handguns. I had some ammunition, but it would have been a running fight. I wouldn't have got them all. They had plenty of cover in that building, and some open distance I'd have to cover that might make things difficult for just one man. It seemed like a bad idea, though now I'm sort of wishing I had tried them, just to see how things would have worked out. I could have gone back to the car and got some long-range firepower, but I figured I ought to get the lay of the land first. I did see some interesting shit, though."

Booger went to work on the cereal. We watched him eat. He ate like it was his last meal, or the last one he wanted. After a couple of minutes he took the cereal box and poured more in the bowl, added milk. He picked a strip of bacon off the plate and ate it like a mongoose swallowing a snake.

"I was watching, counting those motherfuckers," he said, wiping his hands on his pants. "I could see lights through the windows on the building, and now and again I could see someone go past the window. I didn't know what they were doing there, but after a while a couple of women came out laughing, got in a car with a guy and he drove them away. I guess it was a pipe-laying session inside.

"Then this black Suburban drove up and a man got out—"

"What did he look like?" I said.

Booger described him. It was a general description, but with the Suburban added in, I knew it was the guy who I had hit with the stick and tied his shoestrings together. He had worked himself free, way I figured he would. I said, "It's the guy I told you about. The one I hit with the stick."

"You want me to tell this, or what?" Booger said.

"Sure. Sorry."

"So this guy gets out, and he runs up to the building and goes inside, and after about five minutes they all come out. Or a bunch of them do. Maybe someone was still inside, I don't know. But a bunch come out, and there's these two with them, guys in charge. You could tell by the way they carried themselves, like they were hot shit on a stick. They're the ones I think you got the trouble with, an older guy and a younger one. From a distance they looked something alike."

"Sounds like them," I said.

"They push this guy around, the one who came up in the Suburban, and then the older man, the one in charge, knocks him to the ground with his fist, then this other guy in a black leather jacket with a kind of fucked-up head, comes up and pulls a pistol and shoots him right between the eyes.

"That would be Kevin," I said.

"Next thing, most everyone goes inside, except the shooter and one other man. They carry the body to the Suburban, throw it in the back. The shooter drives the Suburban out of there and the other guy follows in one of the other cars."

"They killed him because he fucked up," I said. "I got the best of him, and they killed him for it."

"One less," Booger said. "I counted eight, counting the guy they popped. That leaves seven that I saw, so we know we got that many. But then one more got added."

"How's that?" I said.

"A guy showed up. He came in a regular car, a Chrysler, had on a coat, but when the coat swung open the lights around the place flashed on a badge on his chest. I could see a gun on his hip. A cop."

I described Lieutenant Ernest and Sergeant Allen, knowing neither wore uniforms or badges, but thinking it was possible. Booger said, "Nope. This guy was small. He had on a fedora, but he had a uniform on under the coat, like maybe he'd been in a hurry and hadn't totally undressed, wanted to keep that gun handy. I didn't get a good look at him, but he wasn't fat like your one guy, and he wasn't tall like the other you described. He was a little guy, kind of stocky more than fat. He walked funny, like maybe he had something wrong with his foot. That ring any bells?"

"No," I said.

"Well, one thing is for sure, one cop is in with them. Here's how I see it. This cop, or cops, if more are involved, what they'll do is they'll set it up so you're watched, but the watcher will be one of them, or several of them, and at some point there will be a break-in, and the cops won't know about it, how it happened, or that's how they'll tell it, considering it will be one of them or more than one of them that does the breaking."

"And I get shot with a cold piece they have, and they claim the shooter got past them. They did what they could, but they were too late."

"I think that's how they'll play it," Booger said. "That won't be all of it. I figure they'll do it like that, and then it'll be the rest of your family, because they know who was in the car that ran over your neighbor too. It might take time, but they'll get to all of you. Which means, of course, you want to do this right, we got to get them all,

75

clean them up like sweeping a rat's nest out of the attic."

The day went by slowly, and after a while Cason went out and got in his car, still wearing the same clothes, and drove off. It would just look like he had come over to visit and had stayed the night. Cops were watching, they'd know I said an old army buddy was maybe going to show up. They could figure who that was and how things were anyway they wanted. It didn't matter. If they figured it was one of the bad guys, then maybe they'd stop him and talk to him. But as I looked out the window and watched Cason drive away, it certainly didn't look that way. I eyed both ends of my street, across the way where another street met the one in front of our house. If the cops were out there, they were disguised as mailboxes or my neighbor's cars.

I dropped the curtain and went back to being nervous and anxious and feeling as if I were inside a bad dream I couldn't wake up from.

Booger found a book I had in the living room, a novel, and sat and read. I didn't know he could read. I was beginning to realize Booger was a complicated sociopath. It was odd to see him there on the couch, an unlit Christmas tree sitting in the corner. I thought about the presents that were stored in the closet, and that we would be putting them under the tree and opening them come Christmas morning. If we were still alive.

I took a shower, and since we agreed we didn't want any radios or TV on to keep us from hearing what we might need to hear, I tried to read something myself, but mostly I just walked around the house like a decapitated ghost looking for its head. Somewhere during that day we ate lunch, and then about six that afternoon a phone rang. It was a phone Booger had, a burner. He answered it. He listened for a moment or two, said, "Yeah," and then came into the hallway where I was standing.

"That was Cason," he said.

"Won't they trace that phone to here?" I asked.

"Not this one," he said. "They don't even know to look for a call to it. It's clean, and I'll probably use it for another call or two, then get rid of it. Besides, if it came to it, if they were to trace it, I'd just say it's my phone and Cason has the number. That he's the one put you onto me as a bodyguard. I got excuses out the ass for why he might call me."

"What's the news?" I asked.

"Cason said he'd been working his news sources, and from what he can tell, Ernest and Allen are clean cops, good cops, and they've come down on Anthony before, back when he was a petty criminal. They were tough on the guy whose place the Anthonys took. He said it doesn't look like they're in on shit. "

"Guess I could be wrong," I said, "but I don't like the way those cops kept warning me off."

"Maybe they were just trying to watch for your skin," Booger said. "I don't know. I don't understand that kind of thing, really. I don't like cops. I don't like anyone in authority of any kind. Except me, of course. I'm my own authority."

I went in the kitchen to have something to do and poured myself a glass of juice. Booger asked for the same and I poured him a glass. We sat at the table, and I finally let what was on my mind come out. "Booger, I got to ask. You say you'd kill pretty much anyone?"

"I got to have a reason, but it doesn't have to be in depth. Sometimes you just got to ask, and if there's money, and if I'm bored, well, I can sign on. You asking for a reason?"

"These guys, the Anthony pair, the men working for them, you'll try and kill them because Cason asked?"

"Yeah. I thought I'd get a small bodyguard fee from you as well, just for the hell of it. That's good insurance anyway, like Cason said. In fact, you ought to write me a check pretty damn quick."

"What if it was me, and they hired you to kill me?"

"I'd kill you."

"So you could change sides?"

"No. I gave Cason my word. I wouldn't go back on my word. I said I'd kill them if it came to it, and I will. Next week, someone wanted you dead and paid me money, I might kill you. Well, all right, I wouldn't. Cason says you're a friend. But I make few distinctions. But if I sign on, if I'm riding for the brand, I try and keep riding for it."

"Why are you so close with Cason?"

Booger sipped his juice. "I don't know. I just like him. I think he reminds me of my brother, somehow. My brother is dead. He got caught stealing a car and the cops chased him. He flipped the car. Thing is, and I'd deny it, I was in the car. I got away after it was flipped. He didn't. He couldn't. He had a steering wheel through him. Cason, a lot of times he reminds me of my brother. Way he talks, or something, even the way he moves. He doesn't look a thing like him, but it's something. Or maybe it's just me that thinks it's something."

I nodded, decided not to pressure the question after that. I was afraid I might talk him into turning on me, and maybe even Cason. It was impossible to figure what made Booger tick. Maybe, if in some way I could know, the truth would drive me mad.

I wrote out Booger a check for a thousand dollars, which was a good chunk of change, but the thing was, I wasn't in any mood to be stingy, considering the circumstances. It was nice to have it on record. We hung around all day, talking a little, but mostly changing rooms, sometimes together, sometimes not. I even took a nap for a while. When I got up I asked Booger if he needed to rest for a bit, but he waved me off and kept reading the book he'd gotten off our shelf.

About dark, Booger and I were sitting in the living room, no lights on in there, only the kitchen light was on in the house. It lit the hall a little, the space between kitchen and carport, and that was it. We figured the light would be where they went, and we wouldn't be there. Anyway, Booger was sitting there quietly on the couch, no longer able to read in the dark. He had his hands on his knees and was very relaxed, not moving. I couldn't hear him breathe. I had to keep catching myself to stop bouncing my leg up and down. I didn't know exactly what it was we were waiting for. While we were sitting there Booger lifted his head, said, "Someone's outside."

"You sure?"

"Of course I'm sure," he said.

He got up, reached under his coat and brought out a nine and held it by his leg. He went to the living room window and gently peeled the curtain aside just a little bit, looked out. He waved me over. I took a careful look. It was a bald guy. He was wearing a long coat, but I could see his badge on his chest, his gun on his hip. He was holding something under his coat by pressing his right arm to his side.

"Know him?"

"The dispatcher from the police department," I said.

Booger walked to the wide gap doorway that led into the hallway and stood there waiting. I came up beside him. He kept his voice low, said to me, "When he knocks, cross into the kitchen and come to the opening to the hallway from the other side, near the front door."

Suddenly the doorbell rang.

"Okay," Booger said, "doorbell, not a knock. Ask who's there, but don't stand in front of the door. You do, it won't go well for you."

"What the shit, Booger? It's a cop."

The bell rang again.

"You go where I told you, and you speak out loud near the front door, but not in front of it, and you ask who it is. Go."

I went. It took me only a few seconds to end up where Booger said for me go. The bell rang again.

I said, "Who is it?"

"Police department," a voice I didn't recognize said. "I'm protection detail."

I glanced up the hallway at Booger. He was barely showing from the living room. He leaned out and shook his head.

"What detail?" I said. "There's not supposed to be one yet."

"The Lieutenant thought we should go ahead and start, case word had got out, you know, to Pye Anthony. You standing in front of the door?"

I thought that was an odd question. I looked at Booger. There wasn't a lot of light, but I could see him nod.

"Yes," I said, though I wasn't, and in that moment I remembered what Booger had said about seeing a cop out at Anthony's, one that didn't match the description of the two I'd given him, and in that delayed instant I knew for certain who the rogue cop was.

And in that same moment of realization the door exploded.

Twenty

There was a splintering sound along with a blast of thunder. My ears felt as if they had collapsed inside, and then there was a bit of street light through the door, from the hole that was now in it, and an instant after the explosion, Booger stepped into the hall and cut loose with his nine-millimeter, knocking fist-sized holes around the already existing canyon of a hole that had been made by the blast.

I don't know exactly how many times Booger fired, but I heard a kind of yell, and then a thud, and then Booger came down the hall and opened the door and I stepped out beside him. Trying to crawl down the walk was the dispatcher from the cop shop, leaking blood like oil from a busted transmission. He didn't crawl far before he said, "Fuck," and lay on his stomach with his face on the concrete walk. He didn't say anything else. The blood kept pooling around him. Near the front door was a sawed-off double-barrel shotgun. The air smelled of gunpowder.

Booger said. "I think I hit him just about every shot. I can't believe that motherfucker crawled that far."

He went outside and bent down over the dead man, said, "Ah, he had on a vest. Didn't help. Less impact, I guess, but it got through. Got him once in the neck, too. That was the kill shot, I think. You go in and call the police."

"I don't think that's such a good idea," I said. "They just tried to kill me."

"It's exactly the right thing to do," Booger said.

I wasn't so sure, but to tell you the truth, I didn't know what the right thing to do was. I did know Booger had kept me from being cut in half from a double-barrel shotgun blast.

It was the longest twenty minutes I can remember, and I wasn't sure how it was going to be when they got there; how they would take my bodyguard killing one of their own. Booger had come in the house and put the nine on the kitchen table. He went to the refrigerator and took out the plastic bottle of juice, screwed off the cap and drank straight from it, gulped until it was finished.

"Ahhh," he said, and threw the bottle in the trash. I wasn't in the frame of mind to tell him we recycled. He said, "You and me ought to go out front and wait on them."

Booger took the burner phone, went out back and did something with it. When he came back, he locked the door, plucked the nine from the table and led the way outside through the open front door, as far as the doorway anyway. I followed like a duck. We sat in the open doorway like we were just there to enjoy the night. Neighbors were coming out of houses, though no one was brave enough to cross the street or go any farther than their porch. I didn't blame them. Had I looked outside and seen two men sitting in front of an open door with a hole in it about head height and a bleeding dead man on the concrete walkway, I would have been hesitant as well.

Booger placed his gun on the cement walk, said, "There's a firefly. I haven't seen one of those in years."

Twenty-One

It was kind of a haze after that. We heard a siren, and then we heard more sirens, and then there were lights, the curb filled up with parked police cars, and then the yard filled up with policeman. They took Booger's gun and put us on the ground and handcuffed us and took us and put us in a police car.

Lieutenant Ernest showed up, got in the front passenger seat and glared back at us through the wire grating. After a few minutes Sergeant Allen showed up and sat in the driver's place and looked back at us too.

I told them what happened, how I had hired Booger to protect me, that I knew him from the army. All of this was just to reinforce what I had already said to Ernest. I told them what the dispatcher had said outside the door, about how he had been sent, how I had stepped aside just in time, and then there was the shotgun blast, Booger putting him down, self-defense, the whole nine yards, minus only a few things, like my trip with Kelly out to the Anthony construction site, the threat and so on. I didn't want to tell them about that. I thought if I did they might tip Anthony off if they were in on it, and if they weren't, they might try and have a talk with him, maybe find a reason to arrest him, and that would have the same results for me. He and his son had to be cut completely out of the picture. I didn't doubt that anymore.

After a while, Ernest got out of the car and came around and opened the door and took the handcuffs off of us, but didn't ask us to get out of the car. He said, "Sorry. It's routine. And you got to understand, you killed one of our own."

"And if he had killed me, had Booger not been here," I said, "he would have showed up at work tomorrow and I'd be an unsolved murder."

Ernest closed my door, went back and got in his place on the front passenger side again. He looked back at us. "I suppose that's true."

"This is why your department protecting me isn't all that satisfying," I said, rubbing my wrist where the cuffs had been.

"We have been on him for a while," Allen said. It was the first time he had spoken. "We just weren't sure."

"Hell of a way to find out," I said.

"I didn't think he was a bad cop," Ernest said. "I'm still finding it hard to believe."

"Believe," I said. "He was on Anthony's payroll, and he was sent to get rid of us. He knew about me fingering Will, and he was going to pose as my protection, kill me, head to the house, and be out of the neighborhood before anyone knew what happened. No telling what might have happened to my family afterwards."

"Your wife didn't see Will driving the car," Ernest said. "Your daughter wasn't here. That might have been the end of it."

"That's comforting. Personally, I'm not sure I believe he would have quit there. Kelly could say she saw who I identified at the station, and so on. Forgive me if right now your opinion on these matters isn't particularly inspiring."

"Look," Ernest said. "I'm sorry. I hate it. I liked Fred ... That's his name, the dispatcher. Fred Rutter. I had no idea. He seemed all right. He'd been with the department awhile. Had a bit of a bum leg from an accident on the job, became a dispatcher. Sergeant here suspected someone in the department had been leaking things to Anthony for a while, the boss before him. He was certain it was Fred. I wasn't. I was wrong. I feel like shit in every kind of way possible."

"That's why we were both a little reluctant to push you into testifying," Allen said. "We thought someone in the department might be leaking information, and we didn't want to be the ones that signed your death warrant."

"The sergeant thought that," Ernest said. "I was being cautious, but I thought it was a crock. Now, I know better. Some things you just don't want to believe."

Well, it went on like that for a while, a lot of rehashing of the same thing, apologies, and so on. After that, they took us down to the station for some paperwork, recording out version of events with us in separate rooms, and then they took us back to the house. They kept Booger's nine for evidence, to prove it was the gun and that the gun was legal, which it was. When we got home the cops went in first, at my request, and looked through the place, and then they let Booger and me go inside.

First thing Booger did was ask me to get my shotgun and shells, and I did. I had the .38 Cason had given me hidden away, and I got that and put it in my pants pocket. Booger took the shotgun. I had a hammer and nails out in the carport storage shed, and I got that and a screwdriver, and we took the closet door off in the bedroom and nailed it over the big holes in the front door. It was ugly and awkward looking, but it made the door more secure and covered the gap the shotgun blast had made. While we were covering it, I realized again that the hole was about where my head would have been had I been standing in front of the door. I thought about how I would have been plastered all over the hallway, and it made me a little sick. Lately, a lot of things were making me sick.

The door repaired, we sat in the living room with glasses of ice tea. "You think they believed us?" I said.

"We told the truth, as far as what happened," Booger said. "So when we were being talked to separately, our stories were the same. I think they believed us from the get-go. I have a license for the gun, am a real bodyguard, you knew me from the army. Pretty obvious their dispatcher came to kill us, and they suspected him anyway. I don't think there's anything to worry about."

I heard a car door slam gently outside and I stood up from my chair.

"It's Cason," Booger said, getting up to pull the curtain back for a peek. "I called him at the police station. No one will think it's weird we called a friend."

"You think the cops are watching, then?"

"Sure. Now they are. They drove out behind us. I see the car across the lot there, parked over by that brown house. Those guys couldn't be sneaky if they were invisible. If they were your bodyguards, Anthony and his men could take the tires off their car and they wouldn't even know it."

Cason touched the bell. I let him in.

"I understand you've had a big night," he said as he came in.

"You could say that," I said.

"My suggestion is we make it a bigger night, with what's left of it," he said.

Booger had come into the hall and was standing behind me, still holding the shotgun. As usual, I hadn't heard him come up.

"That's what I was thinking," Booger said. "I'm all fired up right now, and things aren't going to get better, as I'm sure Anthony has gotten word by now, probably from some other leak, that his man is swimming the Styx. We don't go to them, they'll come to us, and it's best we have the element of surprise. If we do it right, it'll be the fucking elephant of surprise."

"I'm sure you saw the cops down the block," Cason said.

"Oh yeah," Booger said. "Just telling Tom here about them. They might as well have been beating a pan and yelling 'Here we are!'"

"So you're talking about tonight?" I said, as if I didn't really believe it, because on some level I didn't. It was like that for me. I couldn't stop questioning things I knew were going to happen.

"Yep," Cason said. "Now."

"What about the cops?" I said.

"Those yo-yos will be waiting for us when we get back," Booger said. "And if we do it right, they'll never even know we were gone."

Twenty-Two

Way we played it, Cason was just a friend who had come by to visit after our traumatic night, and after thirty minutes he left to go home. Least that's how we hoped the cops would see it. He went out and drove away, but we had already left the house through the back door before he did. There wasn't anyone out back, (so much for ace protection) and the fence around my backyard mostly blocked us, long as we ducked low. We didn't bring the shotgun, but I brought the cold piece, the revolver.

I followed Booger as best I could. Slipping through the fence gate, we went alongside the house, eased behind the carport storage shed. We strolled between two houses with Christmas tree lights glowing in their windows, and came out on a back street and walked up that a bit. That's when Cason drove up. Booger got in the front passenger seat and ducked down and I lay in the back seat. I felt a little silly doing all that, but after about fifteen minutes, Cason said, "You can sit up now."

When I did I saw we were traveling out of town, heading out to the country, and I knew sure as hell where we were going.

"We're going to fight them all with my pistol?" I said.

"Oh no, no, no, silly boy," Booger said. "No, no. Not just with the pistol."

"I have a trunk full of weapons," Cason said.

"I put them there," Booger said. "Handguns, long guns, and an axe. We're ready for anything up to an angry hippopotamus, and one of them too, if it's having an off night."

Twenty-Three

We came up behind a pickup truck.

It was the white pickup that had been at the cabin in the woods in Arkansas. The cabin where Kelly, my mother, and Sue were supposed to be waiting. But it was the same truck. I could tell by the rust and the way the license plate was bent up. When I saw it in front of us, going along at a speedy clatter, I wanted to think I was wrong, damn sure hoped I was. I was about to say what I thought when Booger said, "Goddamn it. That truck—"

"It's the one at the cabin," I said, filling in what he was about to say, or something close to it.

"Your goddamn wife," Booger said. "She was supposed to stay put."

"Maybe it just looks like the truck," Cason said.

"No, that's the fucking truck," Booger said.

I could see three shapes in our headlights. I knew the head of the person in the middle as surely as if she were in the car with us. It was Kelly.

"I don't understand," I said.

"I'll tell you what it is," Booger said. "I'll tell you how people think that don't think, but follow what they call their heart, like a fucking muscle that pumps blood has sense and can make good plans. She decided she had left you to the wolves and she couldn't take it. My guess is the daughter and the mother are fine, up there in the woods, and she came back to be with you. To comfort you.

And these fuckers, they were sort of backup to the asshole I killed tonight. When all those cop cars starting coming, they started easing out, and you know what, the road back into town crosses this one, and as fate would have it—"

"Shit," I said. I knew the rest. They had seen Kelly in the truck. It was a million to one, but they had recognized her, had run her off the road, or blocked her path, or some such thing. However it was, they had her. I hoped to hell Booger was right and Kelly had left Mom and Sue behind, left them safe.

"Someone that stupid," Booger said, "we ought to let them have her."

I don't even remember pulling the thirty-eight, but the next moment I had the revolver stuck in Booger's ear. "Shut up!" I said. "Shut the fuck up."

Booger laughed at me. "You ain't going to shoot me, my man. Me and Cason here, we're all you've got."

"It's the way you're talking, Booger," Cason said. "It's offensive. You got to treat a man's wife like you would a fine new weapon."

"You mean keep it oiled," Booger said.

"Not exactly what I meant," Cason said. "Look here, Tom. He's just talking the way he'll talk. We're going to do what we can, and if what we can do is bring Kelly out of this mess, we will."

"If," I said.

"We will," Cason said.

By this time Cason had slowed down and had let the truck get ahead of us by some distance.

"You'll lose them," I said.

"No, I won't," Cason said.

I knew then what he meant. They were taking her to the same place we were heading. The construction site.

Twenty-Four

We could see their taillights when they pulled off the main road and down the road that led to the construction site. We cruised right past that exit, went on for a bit, and Booger said, "There's a little road right up here, a logging road. It ain't much, but you can tuck the car down there and we can come up on the place through the woods, same as I did earlier.

We did that, parked off the road in a little clearing and got out. Cason opened the trunk. It was stuffed with weapons, including an axe.

"I brought us a little bit of this, a little bit of that," Booger said. He took out a rifle and the axe, which was in a kind of sheath. He fastened it to his belt and the handle swung alongside his leg, almost to his ankle. He got out a box of ammo and put it in his coat pocket.

"All good weapons," Cason said. "All simple. Nothing exotic. Harder to trace. Older stuff. Hunting rifles and such. Simple sighting, no telescopes. What we're counting on is Booger's and my shooting being great and yours being good enough."

"I'm not that bad," I said.

"Yes, but I remember you aren't as good as we are, especially Booger, and for you it's been awhile. Me too, actually. Booger, he owns a gun range, so he gets plenty of exercise."

"This is true," Booger said.

"No hard feelings," I said to Booger. "You're right. My wife is an idiot."

"No hard feelings," Booger said. "It don't mean a thing."

I studied the weapons in the trunk. "I'll take a shotgun," I said. "I got my .38."

Booger reached in amongst the weapons and pulled out a knife in a sheath. "Take this, just in case you want to cut everyone's throat."

I took it. It was sheathed. There was a clip on the sheath. I snapped it to my belt. I fished out some ammunition.

Cason took a long gun and two automatic handguns. He snapped the holstered weapons on his belt, one on either hip. "Well, boys, just like the old days over in the Sand Lot. We go in and hope we don't die."

Booger led the way, and me and Cason followed. I swung back and forth between being really mad at Kelly and being proud of the fact she had come back to be with me. Or maybe she was going to make a last-ditch effort to talk me out of testifying. It didn't matter. I had to get to her. I had to save her from those fucking maniacs.

Twenty-Five

We went down through the woods to where the trees broke open and there was the wide red clay section that made up the construction company. It was in a somewhat shallow bowl, more of a saucer, really, and in the saucer was the deep pit with the bulldozer on the rim. There were half a dozen cars parked out front of the large aluminum building and there was a light behind the windows. Beyond the building was another rise, and on that, more woods. The moon was bright enough to give everything a kind of as-seen-through-a-thin-slice-of-cheese look.

The three of us went into a huddle, discussed a few things. Then Booger started moving ahead of us, along the edge of the woods, and finally in line with the pit and the bulldozer. Cason and I eased our way along the column of trees toward the entrance road, and then we broke toward the middle of the lot, stooping, keeping the cars between us and the aluminum building.

We crept up behind the nearest car, a black Suburban, perhaps the one that had been driven by the man who I had hit with the stick and Kevin had killed. Crouching there for a few moments, we moved onward until we were behind the car nearest to the building, a white Cadillac that must have been from the fifties, but looked as if it had just come off the showroom floor.

I lifted up and looked through the driver's-side window glass of the Cadillac, across the way through the passenger side, and examined the aluminum building. A shadow moved behind the window, then went away.

It was then Cason and I heard the bulldozer start up on the hill. That had been Booger's idea. He had a construction company. He knew how to drive a dozer, start them with or without keys, whatever it was you used. The bulldozer was so large and powerful when its engine roared the Cadillac vibrated.

A few seconds later the door on the building opened and a man came out, followed by Kevin and finally Will Anthony. Me and Cason lay down on the ground and looked under the Cadillac at their feet, and while we were watching, another set of legs appeared. That was four that we knew of, and we knew Kelly was inside with some of the others.

The bulldozer started to move. The men outside began to yell at it, as if they could talk it and the driver into shutting the machine off. The bulldozer started down the rise, rolling rapidly toward the aluminum building. The great blade lifted and caught the moonlight. One of the men popped off a shot that rang on the blade, and still the bulldozer came. More shots were fired. More pings and pangs on the blade, and when I glanced over at it, I saw it was really moving. I didn't know a dozer could run that fast.

"Motherfucker," one of the men said, and then the dozer was nearly on the aluminum building, and for that matter, it was nearly on us lying at the edge of the Cadillac.

"Heads up," Cason said, and then we were rushing away and the dozer hit the Cadillac and lifted it up and brought it toward the men in the yard who scattered like geese and then the Cadillac was driven straight into the aluminum building, hard. The front of the building collapsed and the door was knocked off the hinges and thrown inside. I was sick with fear that Kelly would be hurt by all that, but it was a far better way than trying to get past those men and just open the door. The thugs were scattered now, heading left and right at a run. With the Cadillac gone, Cason and I were out there with our asses hanging out, so to speak. That's when Cason lifted his rifle and fired and hit one of the running men in the back of the head, dropping him straight to the ground like a sack of cement.

Kevin ran around the side of the dozer blade, and as Booger was backing the machine off, letting the Cadillac fall, Kevin positioned himself so he could shoot at Booger. I yelled, "Asswipe."

He turned and I cut down on him with the shotgun. A blast from the twelve gauge hit him a little off center and tore into his side and he made a grunt and went to one knee. That's when Booger, still on the dozer, fired a handgun, hit Kevin in the back of the head, knocked his eye out and about half his face off.

I was running by then. A shot went by me, nipping at my coat collar. I leaped and dodged behind the black Suburban. Shots took out the glass and tore through the metal as easily as punching an ice pick through a sheet of paper. But I wasn't hit. That's when I heard Cason's rifle snap. I dropped under the Suburban as I pumped a fresh round into the shotgun's chamber. I saw Cason had hit one of the other men and he had fallen and lay face-down in the dirt. I did a mental calculation. Kevin, two others. That was three down.

Creeping around the rear of the Suburban, I almost had a stroke as Cason came around the back end. I brought the shotgun up, but he shoved it aside with his hand. "Wrong asshole," he said.

We were running together then, dodging toward another car parked to the side of the wrecked building. As we slipped behind the car, Cason said, "I heard someone go out the back. You can check that out or take the building."

"I'll go around back," I said.

I did that, but didn't see anybody. Not at first anyway. Then I saw the Anthonys halfway hidden by the trees, moving like ghosts, going up toward the tree line. They had Kelly with them. They had gotten loose of the building's wreckage. I took to the far right, where there was a run of hardwood. I darted from one tree to another. Glancing up, I saw Kelly stumble and Will jerk her to her feet.

I inched my way on up. Down below I heard more gunfire and Booger yell, "How about coming and getting some of this shit."

More gunfire, and then I heard the distinctive chopping of Booger's axe, the kinds of screams I still hear sometimes when I close my eyes and start to sleep. There is nothing like it; men making a sound so high-pitched the noise could shatter a wine glass.

When I got near the top of the rise, the trees were a little thinner up there, and there was a deer trail, and they were coming along that. I was still pretty well out of sight, behind some brush. They were just below me. As the three came along, Pye in the lead, Kelly next, and then Will, I lifted the shotgun, worrying maybe they were too close together, and that I might hit Kelly. That's when fate worked for me. Kelly and Will lagged slightly, allowing Pye to push ahead. I came out of the brush for a clear shot. Pye saw me. He turned at a crouch. The handgun he was carrying whipped in my direction. He fired, and I fired. His shot whistled past my head. My blast took out his legs and he yelled and hurtled down the hill in my direction, head over heels.

Will saw me, snapped off a shot. By this time I was moving behind a tree. Bark flew from both sides of it as Will began firing at random. That's when Pye, lying on the ground, wounded, but still alive, lifted his hand gun and blasted away. It was a close shot. It struck the oak I was behind and splintered bark. The bark went into my eyes, blinding me for a moment. Luckily, I had already pumped a load into the chamber of the shotgun, and I let it go in Pye's direction.

The general direction was all I needed. When I shook the bark out of my eyes, I saw that what was left of Pye's head could have been stuffed in a thimble with room left over.

Will yelled down the hill, "You son-of-a-bitch. I'm going to kill this cunt. You don't let me pass on by, she's dead."

"You'll kill her anyway," I said. "Let her go and I'll let you go."

"You're lying."

This was true. I was.

"You killed my daddy," he said. It sounded like a petulant kid who had just heard someone say their daddy could beat up his.

I peeked around the lower base of the tree, and when I did, I saw Will was aiming at me. Kelly moved suddenly, knocking his gun hand aside, bringing her shoe down hard across his shin and onto the top of his foot. Will yelled, and that's when he lost it. He hit Kelly in the back of the head with the pistol, knocking her down and out. Down the hill he charged, bellowing like a Confederate Rebel, firing his handgun, which popped twice and then was empty. I heard him say, "Shit. That's about right."

I came out from behind the tree, the shotgun lifted, but damn if Will wasn't already on me, bolting right at me with that empty gun; it was like someone had stuck a rocket in his ass and lit the fuse. He stooped, came under the shotgun barrel before I could figure the situation, knocked it from my hand, and sent us both winding down the hill.

As we rolled, below I heard more gunfire, as well as cussing from Booger, then the falling of the axe and a scream. Seemed there had been more of them than we thought.

Twenty-Six

I made an effort to get my feet under me, but I might as well have promised to lift the world with one hand. Will's elbow had caught me under the chin and my head felt as if it were spinning around on my neck. Everything had narrowed, like I was seeing the world through a cardboard tube.

Finally I rolled over on my side, gathered some of my wits about me, reached for the .38, but I had lost it during my trip down the side of the hill. Will was on his feet, and he kicked me. I took the shot in the ribs, felt something move, but slide back into place. I scrambled on all fours and made it to my feet.

Will pulled a large clasp knife from his pocket, flicked it open and came charging at me. I barely avoided him, and he lunged past. We had both rolled down the hill enough that we were now on level ground, so Will recovered from his miss quickly. I reached for the knife Booger had given me. It was still in place. I pulled it. It was short and sharp and broad.

Will bent low, stabbed at me. I sliced at his knife hand, cut his arm above the wrist. He yelped. It wasn't a deep cut, but it bit him. He slashed at me. I pranced back, avoided it, stepped back in, cut at his elbow as he tried to make a back swing. It was a hit, but his coat saved him from a good, deep slice. He screeched, backpedaled, and then I saw his eyes light up. He was standing on my .38 and knew it. He threw his knife at me. I barely dodged. He reached down to grab the gun. A shadow came up behind him, and with the shadow came movement and a sound like someone breaking a rack of pool balls.

It was Kelly. She had picked up the shotgun, snuck down the rise without either of us noticing her, and now she had hit Will with the stock of the shotgun in the back of the head. He fell to his hands and knees, not having gotten hold of the revolver. I rushed over and shoved him on his back with my foot.

He gave me an addled look. "Don't hurt me."

"You threatened me and my family."

"I give up."

"I don't care," I said.

Kelly walked away briskly.

Smooth as if I were merely drawing a line on paper, I squatted down and cut Will Anthony's throat.

Twenty-Seven

As I went down the hill with Kelly, she said, "You did what you had to do."

"I did it, that much I know."

I was shaking as if I were immersed in ice.

"I came back," she said. "I shouldn't have. But I did. I thought if something happened to you, then it should happen to me too. I didn't like to think you might not live and the last thing you would think of me was what a chickenshit I was."

"I was happier when I knew you were safe," I said.

"And I was unhappy being away from you."

"Mom and Sue?"

"They're fine, though now we have to drive to Arkansas and get them."

At the bottom of the hill Booger had the axe and he was chopping dead bodies as hard and fast as he could. It was sickening. Kelly bent over and vomited, said, "Oh, Jesus."

Cason was looking away from Booger, his hands quivering.

I said, "Is that necessary?"

"He thinks it is," Cason said, "and I advise you to let him have his fun."

"Fun?" I said, turning away, hearing the axe chop.

"For him it is," Cason said. "It rids him of frustration."

When Booger was through chopping—and I'm not sure how he decided he was done, perhaps exhaustion—he got the bulldozer and used it to push the bodies, the crunched up building, all the cars and their weapons, into the big pit. He ran the dozer over it, smashing it all down flat. When that was done, he started pushing dirt on top of it all. It was mid-morning when he finished and we hiked through the woods to Cason's car, the smell of pine sap and evergreens filling our noses.

I wondered about the cops in our neighborhood, our protection. I wondered how many times they might have changed shifts, if they had called our house, or knocked on the door, though they might not have been too eager to do that after they saw what Booger had done to one of their own, traitor or not.

We ended up at Cason's place in Camp Rapture. There he had me and Kelly shower to get rid of blood and gunfire residue. Kelly took her shower with me. We got soaped up and clean, but we got something else done, too, and I have to admit that something else relieved more tension than the warm water.

Out of the shower, Cason had laid clothes out on the bed for us. Shirt and pants and shoes, clean underwear, and socks for me. They were a good fit, as he and I were close to the same size. For Kelly, he had some women's clothes. It didn't surprise me he had them. Cason was the kind of guy that would have quite a few of those left over at his place.

Dressed, we went into the kitchen. Cason was cooking steaks and grilling some vegetables alongside it on an electric grill. He said, "Booger will be back in a little while, about the time this is done, I figure. He went to dispose of the weapons we used."

As Cason predicted, Booger showed up shortly after the steaks were done, and we ate well. I had a beer with the food, and then I was so exhausted I could hardly hold my eyes open. I lay down on the couch, and Kelly lay in my arms, and just before we drifted off to sleep, I heard Booger say, "They're so cute, aren't they?"

I thought he might have been sincere.

It was newly dark when we were awakened by Cason. We went down to the car with him and Booger, and he drove us the back way to our place in Laborde, leaving us a block from it. Booger got out with us, and Cason drove off.

It was dark, but there was enough in the way of street and house lights to see by. We snuck back to the house the way Booger and I had gone out. Only one dog barked, and by that time we were in among some ornamental trees our neighbor grew, then through the carport and the fence gate, the backyard, and into the house.

I checked the phone messages.

None. No cops had called.

"You can't be seen," I said to Kelly.

"No," Booger said. "You can't. Won't be long and we'll be hearing from the law."

He was right. About nine that night I got a call. It was from Lieutenant Ernest.

"That problem you had," he said. "I want to come over and talk to you about it."

"Had," I said.

"Yeah," he said. "I'll explain."

"All right," I said.

Kelly hid in our bedroom. Booger and I sat in the living room and waited.

"You think he's going to try and finish things for Anthony?" I said.

"Nope. No profit for him there now. And I think he's the straight dope. I think he was merely trying to take care of you, in his own cowardly way."

If that was the case, I didn't see it as cowardly.

When Ernest arrived he had Allen with him. They knocked on the door, didn't ring the bell. I let them in. They came and sat at the kitchen table with me and Booger.

Ernest said to Booger, "I got to ask you to let me talk to Tom here in private, if that's okay?"

"That's peaches," Booger said, and went outside to the carport.

"There's been a development," Ernest said. "Someone went out to the construction company, probably one of Anthony's men, and he found the building out there was gone, and the pit was filled up, and this someone made a call in about it."

"What pit?" I said, trying to be casual.

Ernest explained to me there was a pit there where the construction company dug gravel from time to time. A bulldozer was parked where the pit had been. He said the dirt had been moved recently. Real recently, like last night."

"There's a big crew out there right now," Allen said. "They got lights, several bulldozers and the like, and they're digging."

"I don't think I follow," I said. I thought I sounded very convincing.

"It seems someone might have killed the people out there and pushed the building down with the bulldozer, shoved everything into the pit, cars included, and filled it in," Allen said. "I don't know why they would do that, fill it in. They were bound to think we'd look. I was figuring they might have seen it as funny, or maybe they thought no one would look for a while."

"Wow," I said. I knew he was trying to get me to say I might know something about what went on out there, but I wasn't biting.

"Okay, here's the thing," Allen said, dropping the cagey act. "We've actually had the pit dug out. There were bodies buried there. Fresh ones. Chopped up with a machete or an axe or something."

"I'll be damned," I said.

"Yeah," Allen said. "It's a mystery. You have any idea about something like that?"

I shrugged. "Me? Hell no. That's not my line of work, thinking about stuff like that. I'm mystified." I tried not to get to the next part too quickly "When you say bodies, are you suggesting that among those were one or both of the Anthony folk?"

"That is what we're suggesting," Ernest said. "Both of them. Someone had cut off the elder Anthony's head and stuck someone's dick in his mouth. Several were missing dicks, so we haven't decided whose dick was whose, so to speak. I'll leave that to someone who is a specialist at what dick goes where."

"So you're telling me there was some kind of turf war or something like that?" I said.

"We don't know what we're telling you besides they're dead," Ernest said. "It's really handy for you, though, isn't it?"

"I suppose it is," I said.

Ernest nodded, said, "For shits and giggles, say you and that big fucker outside went out there to rub them out, took them by surprise, killed them all. That would sure help you out, wouldn't it?"

"It would. But we been here all night. And besides, I own a frame shop. I'm not a professional killer. The dead guys were."

"How about this one," Ernest said. "Say your watchdog left and did it for you?"

"He would have to be some kind of badass to do all that," I said. "And be back here sitting with me, and out there right now, thinking about whatever he's thinking about."

"I should believe it's puppies and kittens did that to them?" Allen said.

"I wouldn't," I said.

Allen chuckled.

"Besides," I said. "Me and him, we been here all night."

"Yeah," Ernest said. "That's what our watchdogs say. 'Course, they were about half asleep when we showed up."

"That gives me pause about how safe we were tonight," I said.

"Doesn't matter now," Ernest said, standing, Allen rising with him. "I was just trying on a few shoes to see how they fit."

"How did they fit?" I said.

"Not that well," Allen said. "Bottom line is it's done."

They started walking toward the door. When they got there Ernest paused, appeared to be studying the job Booger and I had done nailing the closet door over the hole in the original door. But I knew that wasn't what he was thinking about. He turned and looked at me.

"Thing is," Ernest said, "if I thought you or the big guy had something to do with this, thing for me to do would be investigate it. But, I got to tell you, I feel kind of relieved tonight. Some nasty assholes are in the ground. In pieces. I don't miss them. I guess

105

someone does, a dear old mother, a dog, or someone. But I don't."

"Yeah," Allen said. "I'm not that weepy about it either."

"I got to admit," I said, opening the door to let them out, thinking about Kelly in the bedroom, Mom and Sue safe and sound up in Arkansas, "I don't miss them either."

It was a nice night out. The air had changed. The hot had gone out of it and it was turning really cool, starting to be winter. Maybe it would be real Christmas weather. A wind blew across the yard and made goosebumps rise on my arms. At least I think it was the wind. I was all of a sudden thinking about straddling Will Anthony, pulling that knife across his throat.

I shook it off and watched Ernest and Allen stroll down the walk and out to their car. Allen was on the passenger side, which was closest to me. He had his window down. He lifted his hand off the window frame in a slight wave.

I waved back, and as they drove away, I gently closed the door and turned the lock, went to get Kelly and Booger, and turn on the Christmas tree lights.

About the Author

JOE R. LANSDALE is the author of over thirty novels and numerous short stories. His work has appeared in national anthologies, magazines, and collections, as well as numerous foreign publications. He has written for comics, television, film, newspapers, and Internet sites. His work has been collected in eighteen short-story collections, and he has edited or co-edited over a dozen anthologies. He has received the Edgar Award, eight Bram Stoker Awards, the Horror Writers Association Lifetime Achievement Award, the British Fantasy Award, the Grinzani Cavour Prize for Literature, the Herodotus Historical Fiction Award, the Inkpot Award for Contributions to Science Fiction and Fantasy, and many others. His novella *Bubba Ho-tep* was adapted to film by Don Coscarelli, starring Bruce Campbell and Ossie Davis. His story "Incident On and Off a Mountain Road" was adapted to film for Showtime's *Masters of Horror*. He is currently co-producing several films, among them *The Bottoms*, based on his Edgar Award-winning novel, with Bill Paxton and Brad Wyman, and *The Drive-In*, with Greg Nicotero. He is Writer In Residence at Stephen F. Austin State University, and is the founder of the martial arts system Shen Chuan: Martial Science and its affiliate, Shen Chuan Family System. He is a member of both the United States and International Martial Arts Halls of Fame. He lives in Nacogdoches, Texas with his wife, dog, and two cats.

Made in the USA
Middletown, DE
08 May 2015